PRAISE FOR SWEET MEDICINE

"Panashe Chigumadzi's Sweet Medicine is as fresh and bracing as mountain air. It presents us with a memorable gallery of characters, mainly women, headed by the indomitable Tsitsi, who have to negotiate their way around and often confront a patriarchal society. There are choice sequences that are rendered with humour and sensitivity. Written in the tradition of a bildungsroman, the novel grants us the eyes of a young woman with which to look at a society coming to terms with itself."

– Mandla Langa, author of
The Texture of Shadows

"Tsitsi, an intelligent young woman who has been raised to believe that hard work and education pays, finds herself, upon graduation, condemned to a job that barely pays. Her mother's hope, she soon decides that she must make a plan if she is to survive. How Panashe Chigumadzi deftly deals with Tsitsi's decision as a young woman who must make it against all odds is what makes Sweet Medicine a must-read. Through this book and Tsitsi's story, Chigumadzi shows us how a country's political policies, can destroy the very people it's supposed to serve."

– Zukiswa Wanner, journalist and author of *London Cape Town Joburg*

"Sweet Medicine is an exquisitely told story. Chigumadzi is not overwhelmed by the sensitivity and delicate nature of the Zimbabwean narrative but observes and narrates with skilful detachment to personal and public crises as they unfold."

– Tinashe Mushakavanhu,
The Standard (Zimbabwe)

"Written in the wake of Aidoo, Dangarembga and Adichie, Sweet Medicine has a voice and drive all of its own: witty, incisive and thought-provoking, it is a novelistic debut you will find hard to put down."

– Dr. Ranka Primorac, University of Southampton

SWEET MEDICINE

PANASHE CHIGUMADZI

First published by Blackbird Books in 2015
Second, third and fourth impression 2016
Fifth and sixth impression 2017
Seventh impression 2019
Eighth impression 2020
Ninth impression 2021
Tenth Impression (print only) published under license by Rising Action
Publishing Co., 2022

593 Zone 4
Seshego
Polokwane 0742
South Africa
www.blackbirdbooks.africa

ISBN 978-1-998076-32-1

Distributed in North America by Blackstone Publishing

Cover design by Nuno Moreira

See a complete list of Blackbird Books titles at
www.blackbirdbooks.africa

Rising Action Publishing Co.
http://www.risingactionpublishingco.com

BLACKBIRD
BOOKS

RISING ACTION

Kuna Mama, Deddie, Fari
Constants in my life. As you always say, "There are only four of us." In all that you have done, the greatest gift that you have given me is letting me know that I am enough.

PROLOGUE

"You cannot fight an evil disease with sweet medicine," says the n'anga.

The sound of her voice is unexpected. Perhaps it had been the bad network reception that had obscured and forced it into a strong, raspy voice as they shouted to hear each other on the phone before, because it is now soft and reedy.

It is winter, so it is still dark, even at 5 am.

The consulting room is a brick appendage to the n'anga's matchbox house. The early-morning consultation time did not require much negotiating. For Tsitsi, the ungodly hour will conceal this clandestine affair. For Mai Matumbu, it means that she can still be on time for her job as an accounts clerk at the Chitungwiza Town Council.

In the glimmer of light from a small fire at the centre of the room, Tsitsi can just make out the large figure of the n'anga, which feels particularly imposing compared to her own small frame.

Up until this point, Tsitsi has kept her eyes on the floor. As she had been led into the consulting room, she had been guided by the sight of the n'anga's cracked and calloused heels, only taking account of what was sufficient for her to walk without injury. This, to ensure that there would be no vivid vignettes or recollections of the n'anga and the consultation, and that she would only be able to piece together an apocryphal account, which in time she would dismiss as a hallucination or strange dream.

Now, catching a glimpse of the n'anga's chipped red nail polish, Tsitsi is distracted. She squints her eyes at the long, coloured toenails, and feels a sense of doubt creep up on her: what time does any real n'anga have for a frivolous preoccupation with cosmetics? The question overcomes her desire for a no-more-than-hazy recollection, forcing her eyes from the floor. She sees that aside from cowrie shells that decorate the woman's ample breasts, the n'anga is otherwise a plain-clothes traditional healer in a long-sleeved, black vest and pleated, brown, ankle-length skirt. Before her less-than-ceremonial dress can inspire any further doubts of her legitimacy, a cold breeze quickly points Tsitsi to the impracticality of the kind of bare-legged and bare-breasted traditional regalia she might have expected.

She casts her eyes up to the face of the n'anga. Her skin is like varnished pine wood, not the dark charcoal colour she had expected, and although she has dreadlocks, they are neatly pulled back by an elastic band. The woman is not particularly striking or even feral looking, as Tsitsi had expected from her childish imaginings. She looks nothing like an old African hag, so Tsitsi eases herself further into her surroundings. She even remembers that the woman's name is Esther, or rather, Mai Matumbu, but Tsitsi does not want to become overly familiar and so keeps her distance, even with her newfound ease.

She casts her eyes around the dimly lit room, peering into each corner, looking thoroughly this way and that, like an Inspector of Native Schools, feeling the concomitant scepticism of the legitimacy of the operation. But she quickly puts that out of her mind. Even if it is to effect some change by means of a placebo effect, she is indifferent, as long as her ends are achieved.

The n'anga points to a grass mat in front of her calloused feet. Tsitsi obeys immediately and kneels before her. She is at first grateful for the mat: it means she will be able to keep the skirt of her African attire free of soot and therefore unsuspicious. But she realises that the smoke from the small fire burning behind the n'anga will linger on her clothes and she will have to change anyway if she wants to avoid any questions.

She kicks off her right Ferragamo heel after she uses the pointed heel on her left foot to dislodge it, and then uses her freed toes to free her left foot. She shivers slightly as the balls of her delicate feet connect with the cold of the polished concrete.

Tsitsi closes her eyes as she feels her heart constrict with both pleasure and pain as she contemplates the n'anga's choice of words on the phone: 'evil disease.'

Pleasure because, yes, that's what it is. An evil disease. The omniscience of the n'anga has ensured a fitting diagnosis. A woman herself, she has likely fought the same disease, so she is well equipped to help Tsitsi.

Pain, because of what she fears the evil disease can take away and destroy if it is not eradicated quickly enough.

"I'll give you something—something strong," words spoken firmly, reinforcing Tsitsi's sense of the n'anga's omnipotence.

The n'anga kneels down on the mat.

In Tsitsi's imagining ...

From the small fire, smoke curls up in wisps through the winter air as the n'anga begins huffing, letting out infrequent shrills, her eyes rolling back, her head upturned as if to the heavens. Her body shakes violently, causing the cowrie shells around her ample breasts to rattle noisily as she invokes the spirits, beginning her mixture of divination and alchemy. The line is indistinguishable to Tsitsi. Only at this time does she care for the distinction between the healing powers of a n'anga and the divinatory powers of a svikiro. The difference is important as she seeks a herbal remedy to her problems. She is not yet ready to enter that other realm of her own accord.

In reality ...

From the small fire, smoke curls up in wisps through the winter air as Mai Matumbu initiates conversation with Tsitsi, further probing the details of her dilemma. As Tsitsi speaks, the woman nods thoughtfully, almost reassuringly, and reconfirms her initial diagnosis of an evil disease.

Tsitsi winces as the woman reaches into her bra and produces a razor. Seeing her hesitation, the woman lays a reassuring hand on her shoulder. Although somewhat comforted by the gesture, she still finds herself leaning back involuntarily as the woman moves forward to bring the razor to Tsitsi's chest. She tries to suppress her instinct to pull back, to protect herself and to remain still, but she fails, flinching as her chest smarts where the woman draws beads of blood that drop into a wooden bowl held below her chest. The woman rises to her full height and walks heavily and flatfooted, slowly making her way in a manner that seems uncharacteristic of the supernatural, to the backroom-cum-dispensary formed by old, holed curtains with colour faded from long exposure to the sun.

As the curtains part, Tsitsi is unable to sustain the sense of ease and immediately shuts her eyes tightly as her mind's eye begins to conjure up images of hell: faces of the damned with gaping mouths, revealing jaws with great pointed teeth, seeking victims who are gnashing their teeth in unbearable pain. Whenever Tsitsi was disobedient as a child, her mother —a woman secure in the moral certainties of the Catholic Church—would make her faithful representations of eternal damnation in vivid, certain detail. Mama had only to speak of this and no sooner was Tsitsi flying, weeping, into her open, redemptive arms.

Tsitsi feels her heart constrict again, as the memories and images linger in her mind. She breathes deeply and, once her lungs are filled, holds her breath to stop the spread of the pain.

This is necessary. And so is all that Tsitsi has entangled herself in. For Tsitsi the only solution is to shed her Catholic carapace and take an indefinite leave of absence.

She exhales, opens her eyes and begins to scan the wall behind the threadbare curtain. Nothing. The wall itself is bare, while myriad herbs and plants, interspersed with the odd animal skin or tail, are lined up on the floor. Her view is then obscured by the woman as she returns. Disappointed, Tsitsi fixes her eyes on Mai Matumbu's hands, blemished with burn marks and small scars. She notices the matching chipped-red on the woman's fingernails. This time Tsitsi does not allow herself to be distracted by the trivial detail and quickly dismisses it, reminding herself that this is her last resort.

She watches the woman's hands; one grips a reused glass

jar and a small leather pouch wound with what looks like a blood-dampened thong, and the other a bunch of herbs. Tsitsi is perturbed by the jar's contents: what looks like a shrivelled and pickled body part in some kind of oil. She narrows her eyes at the jar, trying to ascertain whether it really contains a body part. It looks like a hand. She suppresses a gasp as she thinks of the 'muti-murders' that would inevitably crop up in conversations about the notoriously powerful healers in South Africa.

Surely this woman isn't an accomplice to that kind of medieval practice? Maybe it is just a small hand of some animal. A small animal, yes. Yes, an animal—like a monkey. They're quite human-like, aren't they? Yes. It is the hand of a monkey, not a small person.

As Tsitsi reassures herself, the n'anga places the jar in her hand. She is told that it is to eliminate her nemesis. As she grasps the cold glass, Tsitsi feels herself boil into a guilty excitement.

Next, the n'anga places the pouch in her palm. The amorphous shape does not betray its contents and, it seems, her curiosity will not be satisfied because she is forbidden from opening it or she risks losing its power to fix his eyes on her indefinitely.

The n'anga turns her body in order to place a small pot onto the metal stand over the fire and pours water from a bucket into it. "The lights have been gone since last week," she explains as she fans the embers of the fire with an old folded newspaper. But the flames barely lick the bottom of the pot, so she lowers her upper body to the floor and blows furiously into the glowing coals. As the stooped figure breaks into a sweat, the flames become taller, engulfing the pot's bottom. The room is effused with grey smoke, reminding Tsitsi of her not-so-far-away days at the stool beside the fire, and she tightens the dhuku she has tied around her head to keep the smoke from spoiling her Brazilian weave.

Finally, as the water begins to boil, the n'anga drops the herbs into the pot, turning the water a light green colour. It's not long before furious bubbles swim to the surface of the water as it begins to turn into a broth. Satisfied that the herbs have infused enough of their essence into the water, the n'anga grabs the pot's long handle and pours some of the liquid into an enamel cup and thrusts it into Tsitsi's hands. Forgetting that enamel is a good conductor of heat, she nearly drops it.

The steam from the cup carries the rancid smell of the liquid. She shuts her eyes as it penetrates her nostrils. Pinching them closed and casting an uneasy glance at the n'anga, then shutting them tightly again, she gulps the liquid and swallows. The sharp, bitter brew makes her choke initially, but soon an invigorating sensation overwhelms her as the liquid begins to mingle with her blood. Drinking the last of the broth, Tsitsi is reminded of the redemptive effect she felt when she took communion wine. She would always end her prayer once she felt the burn of the wine in her heart, the moment at which she felt renewed and reborn, as if Christ's blood had incinerated the last remnants of her venial sin.

Now, through the burning sensation she feels in her heart as the liquid diffuses itself, this communion is lighting up something quite different. It is inducting her into a new world, what her mother, and she herself, had seen as a false consciousness, blasphemy to be precise. If she had already had her first baptism at the hands of Zvobgo, this was now her second, as she culpably confirmed herself into this other world.

Only because it is necessary and because it is temporary, she dictates to herself once again. Reading the sensation as a gauge of the liquid's potency, Tsitsi is satisfied that she has made a good decision in seeking out a female n'anga. Female empathy, that woman-to-woman kind, allows for immeasurably increased potency. She, this stranger, perfectly understands Zvobgo's disease. The weakness in men a unifier between these two women. At this thought, Tsitsi again feels a deep, guilty excitement as if she has come to a forbidden fruit.

But the thought of forbidden fruit makes her think of her mother once again. Is Mama not happy that she no longer has to worry about issues of bread? That she now has the freedom to be consumed by matters of the word? That she now only has to concern herself with her spiritual life?

Besides, praying had not yielded tangible results for Tsitsi, at least not quickly enough. She needs guarantees.

Tsitsi struggles to her feet and thrusts US$500, half her weekly allowance—a tenth of which already had gone to her tithe—into the n'anga's hands. The woman licks her finger and flips through the notes, counting them twice before snapping an elastic band around them and planting them behind the fabric of her bra.

A cold gush of air quickly ushers Tsitsi out of the consulting room, and pushes her into a gentle run as she hikes her skirt up to avoid the ground, to the rusted iron gate at the front of the n'anga's house.

The stench of concentrated life, standing water and open drains hits her nose. She has the urge to pinch her nostrils closed, like someone who has never lived in a location, but resists and instead holds her breath. She makes her way past the hawkers assaulting her ears with their calls to buy their goods, cheap-cheap.

Finally, she reaches her Land Cruiser and slips a searching hand into her handbag for her keys. Once in the safety of the Land Cruiser, Tsitsi checks that the jar and the pouch are safely inside her handbag. Satisfied, she exhales. She fastens her seatbelt, switches on the ignition and releases the handbrake.

1

Although Sekuru Dickson was outside on the veranda, Tsitsi hooted as she parked the Land Cruiser outside the wrought-iron gate of Mama's house. She was there to make her weekly delivery of groceries and other supplies—light bulbs, clothing and her mother's tablets—unavailable at the local shops, cash or not. Zvobgo frequently questioned her insistence on making the delivery herself when there were drivers at her disposal. He had even offered to have one of the drivers assigned to Mama. The driver would be responsible for delivering the groceries from Tsitsi and Zvobgo's Highlands house to Mama's Kuwadzana house, ferrying her to and from mass and her Maria Hosi Yedenga Guild meetings at Kuwadzana's Holy Trinity Catholic Church, the hospital and to wherever else she—and Sekuru, for that matter—wanted or needed to go (although Sekuru's trips to the bar would, of course, be limited). The offer was declined by both women: by Mama for the unspoken reason that she wanted to depend on Zvobgo as little as was humanly possible given the circumstances, and by Tsitsi because the current arrangement offered her a functional pretext to visit her mother.

Sekuru Dickson was startled by the sound of the car's horn, dropping the cane walking stick that propped him up as he sat on the boulder outside Mama's room, absorbing the sun, listening to his radio that played 'Mugove,' his favourite song by Leonard 'Karikoga' Zhakata, or, for that matter, any artist.

Realising that it was Tsitsi at the gate, he hoisted himself to his feet, and walked clumsily towards the gate. As he walked, Sekuru sang along with Karikoga just as he began his plea against the merry Sungura beat that belied the message.

Together, forming a formidable band that would have surely rivalled the Zimbabwe All Stars, Karikoga and Sekuru mused again, with unrelenting urgency each afternoon, why the good Lord hadn't given them their fair share of heavenly gifts while still on Earth. Sekuru sang his favourite verse with the urgency of someone who was indeed about to keel over and indeed never see his fair share.

Over the last few years, Sekuru had aged dramatically, almost in proportion to the chaos around him. He was wearing his old bowler hat, which cast a narrow shadow over his leathery forehead. His old, oversized khaki jacket made his shoulders look abnormally wide, and, together with his hat and lopsided walk, made him look like a scarecrow chasing after menacing birds in the field. The jacket was part of the uniform he had worn as a security guard at a bank in town, his one and only job from when town was Salisbury, right up until Harare was no longer the Sunshine City. Tsitsi remembered that, when she was back home from boarding school, he would ask her to visit him at the bank, and of course she obliged because it always meant extra tuck money. "This is my daughter!" he would tell the clerks as he marched her to their counters. "In the not too distant future, you will be receiving orders from her." To this, the male clerks, tracing her nascent curves and ignoring her severe schoolgirl haircut, would respond, "Dickson, this is not a bank boss, this is a beauty queen! This is our future Miss Zimbabwe!"

This was a man who had always been so proud and dignified in his work—so much so that he was always dressed formally in his old uniform, even without occasion. So, of course, he was also wearing his cherished imitation-gold tie-clip, which had kept his striped maroon tie from flapping as he trotted to and from the bank counters on the orders of the bank clerks, and today kept it from flapping as he hurried to open the gate for Tsitsi.

Sekuru Dickson opened the gate, raising his arms to greet her. It was funny to think that in the past he had threatened to drag Tsitsi out of Zvobgo's house and impound her. But with the proliferation of zeroes and the attendant queues, his resistance eased and he dared not bite the hand that fed him, despite the hand having delayed paying roora for his Dear Daughter.

"Mwanangu, you have come! Tigashire, tigashire!" he sang as he opened the door of her Land Cruiser.

"Muchigashirei, Sekuru?" she exclaimed, reciprocating his enthusiasm as he almost toppled her, grabbing her forearms in his embrace. "Is Mama here?" she asked in English as she smoothed her dress.

"Ah, that one? She's here. Where else would she go?" Then, answering the question himself, he continued, "Schools are closed, there are no church meetings today and there is still some time before the evening mass. She is inside the house."

Tsitsi laughed. She knew her mother would be home. When she was not at school, the house of the Lord and her own house were the two axes of her mother's existence. She had only wanted to indulge her uncle's love for demonstrating the English he'd perfected at the bank. It was always comical to hear Sekuru in his best English, a show he'd begun in appreciation of her education.

Sekuru and Mama had always been convinced of the superiority of English over Shona, which they felt was a language reserved only for domestic matters, mashopeshope and other not-so-important undertakings. It was certainly not up to the task of articulating any of the demands of the wonderful, modern and important world to which Tsitsi was to ascend all those years ago and now in which she had staked a foot-, or, toehold, depending on whom you asked.

Indeed, Sekuru would say in English, "Tsitsi, my child, you must speak English so well that even Smith himself will have to consult a dictionary."

From the time she was a child, they had taken a keen interest in her schooling. Whenever she had returned from school, there was a flood of questions. Had she behaved well? What lessons had she learnt that day? How many sums had she got right? What new words could she spell? She was required not to spare any details of the day spent in the classroom where the children would drone as they recited a lesson in chorus and the teacher would scratch her chalk against the blackboard. Mama would listen with a patient smile on her face when she heard that she was doing well and would frown when she heard that Tsitsi was having any difficulty.

Later, when Tsitsi would return from boarding school, her mother would assemble primary-school children to hear how she had done. They would crowd around her, giggling and squealing, bursting with curiosity and admiration for their Big Sister in Boarding, but were always too shy to ask their own questions.

She was going to be a doctor, so she took maths, biology and chemistry. When she was home, not a day went by without Mama or Sekuru speaking of the merits of the medical profession. If they had had access to them, Tsitsi was sure they would have brought home books and brochures on medicine for her to read. They were somewhat disappointed when she then took an interest in economics, but were nonetheless delighted that their daughter would be going to university and thereafter would enter the world of professionals. Professionals. Professions. So many of their life's problems were to be solved in one brushstroke by means of professionalisation.

"I have some parcels—please call Susan to come help us."

"Ehe! Where is that girl?" Sekuru gave a little dance before turning towards the house and summoning the house girl.

"Sisi! Susan! Sisi!"

As Tsitsi opened the boot of the Land Cruiser, Susan quickly emerged to carry the groceries into the house. Her head took a box, and her hand, the one not keeping the box steady, took hold of a plastic bag. Tsitsi picked up a box and carried it with both hands—she was not going to spoil the elaborate style in which she had wrapped her head in her turban-cum-headwrap or gele, as she'd been told it was called. She started for the house but when she sensed that Sekuru Dickson had stayed back, she turned to look. With his walking stick, he gestured for her to come closer. She put her box down and went to his side.

"Tsitsi, mwanangu, you will drop me off in town when you are leaving, nhaika?"

She frowned, "Why, what's there, Sekuru?"

He scratched in his trouser pockets and pulled out a dirty flier, folded haphazardly.

"Oi, Mama," he said as he offered her the paper. He had adjusted the tone of his voice to a reedier one, to make his body seem frailer. Tsitsi's frown grew deeper as she opened the flier and read its contents.Tsitsi felt her face getting hot. How could he, Sekuru, believe in this Professor and Mbuya Gondo? Her eyes narrowed at points eight and twenty-three, and the number one under "MEN ENLARGEMENT CREAM & WOMEN TIGHTENING", which he had underlined.

Even if these two Gondos had these powers, Tsitsi thought, why was Sekuru in any need of performance enhancers? He had no business with his pants down, except to use the toilet or change clothes. And what kind of black spot was this in number twenty-three? What was that supposed to be? Was it invisible? She wanted to ask him. The only thing taking the money that I give you is the hand of the bottlestore owner, she thought but didn't say.

She looked at her uncle's face, her eyes tracing the lines

PROF. & MBUYA GONDO
Diploma, Council for Local and International Medicines, Malawi

FIND THE DOCTORS IN CBD
We also make house calls
Call 0778778099
profgondo123@yahoo.co.uk

1. To betoldall your problems beforeyousay anything
2. Do you want to see your enemies in the mirror?
3. Want to know your future
4. Get married in a shortest time to a person of your dreams
5. Bring back your lost lover in short time possible
6. Win court cases with just natural traditional help
7. Do you want to protect yourself and guaranty safety for yourself
8. Get wealth through spiritual help
9. Do you want to talk your ancestors?
10. Get a job or promotion at work
11. Do you want to cleanse your self
12. Want to win lotto, casino, horses etc, with traditional help
13. Do you want to sell property quickly?
14. Want to get by the help of traditional herbs?
15. Quitalcohol, smoking, drugs& gamblingaddictions with no side effects
16. Want to get inheritance, settlements, you have fought for a long time
17. You want retirement, retrenchment and benefirts?
18. Body pains, diseases & sleepless nights
19. Makeyourpartnerloveyoumoreandstophim\ her from cheating
20. Stop your partner avoiding separating from you
21. Stop quarrels between couples, family, relatives, employees etc?
22. Revenge evil spirits with the help of traditional spirits
23. Do you want to remove a black spot in your hand that keeps taking away your money?
24. Do you want to stop divorce from your partner
25. Increase customer attraction for your busyness
26. Want to remove bad spells, bad luck from homes, people, family or business
27. We also assist on HIV\AIDS signs & symptoms

MEN ENLARGEMENT CREAM & WOMEN TIGHTENING
1. Became a tiger in bed
2. Size(length & thickness)
3. Power(Hardness & strong)
4. Stop early ejaculation, make more rounds & boost sexual feelings

of age that mapped his charcoal leather skin. Silly old man! Such gullibility should have dried up with the last of his youth. The thought made her angry. Even worse, what made him think that she would agree to be his accomplice? He knew Mama would disapprove of this, yet he still felt it appropriate to ask Tsitsi to be involved. She felt the urge to crumple the paper up and throw it into the rubbish heap outside the gate. Why, how could he be so foolish? Work, don't wish, she thought. But his old crooked leg reminded her that the likelihood of that happening was more than a little doubtful.

Instead, he was grabbing at whatever was available in this system that no longer held the old predictable relationship between effort and result as true – that relationship she'd internalised in her childhood after repeatedly hearing her mother command: shanda mwanangu shingirira! She implored her Tsitsi and her students. Work. Persevere. But chaos pummelled the words into themselves and brought a new order, one in which Cunning was King. One where her youth allowed her to be nimble and able to adapt, while his age kept him trapped in a corner.

She was not entirely at ease with her new position of authority that could veto his seniority. It went against her traditional sensibilities. She straightened her brow, folded the sheet of paper and placed the flier in her handbag.

"Sekuru Dickson, you know Mama wouldn't like this." She imagined her mother's lips and the way they twisted in disdain. This was the one thing that her mother would not keep quiet about. To her, any sort of religious indiscretion was the devil. You simply could not pick and choose what was to be followed as and when you felt like it. "You know what she would say: maintain the spirit of prayer and place your problems with Him. Don't waste your time with these things."

She said these words with a keen sense of their futility;

she knew her uncle had no qualms about his religious flexibility.

A broad grin spread across Sekuru's face as he clasped his hands in a gesture of prayer.

"Tsitsi, mwanangu, handidi kunyepaba – you talk a lot of sense. All those years that I took care of you, you were always full of sense. You were such a clever girl. Shuva, unotaura chokwadi. What more could I ask for, when you, my dear child, are here to look after me?" He spoke in Shona as he took off his hat and cradled his head in her breasts. Tsitsi knew he was hinting at a top-up, but refused to respond. "Only a small favour, for looking after you for all of your childhood? Only this one."

He swore to the truth of the singularity of the request by wetting his index finger in his mouth, and then pointing to the sky.

"Horaiti, Sekuru," she sighed, knowing how unrelenting he could be, and prized a few notes from the side pocket of her handbag.

He began his dance of gratitude, clapping cupped hands, "Mazvita! Mazvita, Mama!" he sang as he bent over in deference to Tsitsi before placing the notes in the inner pocket of the old jacket, where he kept his gin bottle. The old boy then continued his dance, imitating the dancers from the Jairos Jiri Band – only it wasn't much of an imitation, because he really did have a physical impairment.

Embarrassed by his act, Tsitsi pulled Sekuru up by his arms and gestured to the house, leaving the boxes for Susan. He knowingly obliged and led her into the small house her mother had bought and steadily extended in the years since her father had died; he had been chased from their home by his brothers. The house was compact with a sturdy frame, like her mother whose own strong bony frame had enabled her to survive some of the worst life can offer. It was not always easy being the daughter of such a woman. Mama placed a premium on containing her problems, swallowing her bitterness along with the blood pressure pills Tsitsi imported for her.

Before she crossed the threshold of the house into the small sitting room, Tsitsi pulled down the hip of her dress, which had ridden up and held her bum in a tight grip.

"Sisi! Did you see what our child has brought for us?" Sekuru asked of his sister as if it were the first time she had brought them anything.

When Tsitsi entered the room, Mama remained seated and silent, only nodding her head in acknowledgement of her daughter and the groceries she brought with her. She sat upright, her small body framed by the oversized maroon armchair. Sekuru had seated himself on the two-seater (or one-and-a-half, as Sekuru sometimes pointed out) adjacent to the armchair, happily positioning himself on the end furthest from Mama, making way for Tsitsi, who eased herself slowly onto the sofa, careful not to drop down, but nonetheless caused her mother's carefully knitted doily to fall.

Mama wore her plain green dhuku, with her green jersey over the white T-shirt tucked into a green-and-white zambia, the wrapper made specially for the Maria Hosi Yedenga Guild meetings by one of the assistants in Zvobgo's office. The uniform was one of the few concessions she had made in accepting gifts from Zvobgo. One she had made by giving in to the pleading of the Women's Guild after Zvobgo had sent his people directly to them to enquire their sizes, measurements and design preferences.

Even in her plain clothes, this primary-school teacher looked regal in the chair. With her cheekbones protruding and her striking dark eyes, she had none of the plainness she tried so hard to achieve in order to keep her from being a distraction to her fellow congregants or being the object of jealousy and hatred as she had often been throughout her life.

To her pain, she had passed those sharp features on to her daughter, whose own cheekbones stood out, uncluttered by the weave hidden by her bright orange gele. Tsitsi's polished ebony skin shone in the same hue as her mother's and was beautifully contrasted against the bright gele. Her matching floor-length West African-style dress, puffed out at her shoulders, was nipped in at the waist and flowed straight down to her ankles to reveal Ferragamo kitten heels, transforming her small, curvy figure into the very kind of distraction her mother had warned her daughter against.

The West African style was the uniform of the politburo wives and so Tsitsi had followed suit to disambiguate herself from a Small House and to match her status as Zvobgo's respectable, albeit unofficial, wife.

Her colours were a loud intrusion against the austere colours of the living room: the off-white of the room interrupted only by portraits of a prayerful Jesus and The Last Supper, an imitation gold clock that had been a wedding gift, the brown-painted cabinet that displayed her crockery set, and the blue doors to Mama and Sekuru's bedrooms.

Moving to the edge of the couch and clapping her cupped hands, Tsitsi began the traditional greeting, something she had come to be grateful for in as much as they were conversational placeholders.

"Makadii, Sekuru?" she asked dutifully.

"Ha-a, ndakasimba, Tsitsi. No problems here, my daughter," he said with a broad smile on his face, clapping his cupped hands in response. "Wakadiiko?"

"Ndakasimba, Sekuru."

She turned to her mother, "Makadii, Mama?"

"Ndakasimba," she said quietly, her hands soon returning to her lap, signalling the return to her silence.

Lingering at the edge of the seat, Tsitsi attempted, "How is church?"

"It's fine."

"How is the Women's Guild?" she asked once more.

"It's fine."

Still at the edge, she turned to her uncle. "And you, Sekuru? How are things? When will you be going kumusha to see your wife and the village? Have you planted yet?"

"Ah," he laughed, waving a dismissive hand, "that one is young! Don't worry about her. She can plough on her own." He turned to face his sister, "Sisi, remember when we used to plough our mother's fields alone? Just the two of us! I'm telling you, Tsitsi, she can do it alone."

The memory amused him so much that the force of his laughter made him cough. Mama only raised her head. Although Tsitsi laughed too, she did sometimes feel that he should go home to the village, like the Khmer Rouge had wanted their people to do. To go back to the halcyon days of a simple agrarian life, instead of the jostle and toil for a precarious toehold in town.

Sekuru's laughter eventually died down and he grew quiet.

"If I help, if I don't help, it's the same. We don't know if anything will come out. Things are always changing; the seasons don't seem to be the same. The rain comes when it wants. It doesn't seem to help to go there any more."

Tsitsi diverted her eyes from Sekuru's and settled them on the gold wedding clock, watching the minute and hour hands coordinate themselves, moving from 3:33 to 3:48 as Sekuru quietly hummed 'Hapana Akafanana na Jesu', rocking gently on the couch and thrumming his fingers on the wooden arm of the chair. She kept her eyes there even when her back began to ache as she kept it upright and maintained her position on the edge of the seat. Her eyes were drawn from the hands of the clock when he switched the TV on and let out a rocket of boyish laughter that ricocheted between the two silent bodies as he amused himself with the sight of two pensive-looking characters in conversation in a Chinese film on ZBC.

Mama kept a cool silence throughout, sitting in a firm position in the armchair, hands placed on her lap. This was not unusual; Mama had always been a quiet person. But this was not the companionable silence they had shared as Tsitsi sat doing her homework by candlelight while Mama ironed the clothes she washed for extra money or when they would peel peas together. It was a silence to withhold judgement. A disciplining silence that Mama had employed when Tsitsi had misbehaved as a child.

On this day Tsitsi began to feel irritated with her mother. If it were not for Zvobgo, she would not have the church uniform or wine at mass, let alone any of the food in the house that she now took for granted. She should be grateful that she didn't have to take the trip to South Africa to buy wares and return to sell them like her fellow congregants and her fellow teachers. She, what's more, was alive. Her life had not been taken on that road, unlike Mai George from next door.

Sometimes Tsitsi wished that Mama would be unreasonably demanding instead of as unexpecting as she was. She sometimes wished she were one of those mothers who laid claim to their children's success, like Chiedza's mother had done. Mai Chiedza had had a stroke, which she blamed on the witchcraft of her neighbours jealous of the fact that she had a daughter to look after her in her old age and in the difficulties of the current times, and so she moved from her home in Chitungwiza to live with Chiedza in her flat in town.

She had felt everybody, including Chiedza, was in on this terrible conspiracy, which really was a failed attempt on her precious life. She felt everyone around her, especially Chiedza whom she had blessed with life, owed her attention, pity and service.

She had expected instant service from her daughter, complaining openly and incessantly of neglect. When she wasn't complaining directly, she flung sarcastic barbs like stones from a catapult, lamenting the way in which she, an old woman, was being abused by these young people.

No, Mama was not like Mai Chiedza who had become childlike, playing a game where she would be relaxed until, seeing her daughter – even if only catching her in the periphery of her sight – would immediately become an invalid, sighing and wishing aloud that her body would not play tricks on her and would allow her to do things for herself.

It was not enough that Chiedza ensured that all her favourite treats, such as yoghurts, biscuits and cornflakes, were there for her on demand or that she had hired a young, and costly, physiotherapist from Parirenyatwa to help her regain movement on the left side of her body, or that she tended to her hand and foot whenever she was home.

When she died, Chiedza simultaneously cried the grief of one finding themselves an orphan in the world and cried for the relief from an unrepayable, unreasonable debt.

Instead Mama had no demands.

Today Mama, as usual, did not reciprocate the questions. Her face was impassive, as if she couldn't hear their conversations. She said nothing, held back by her acknowledgement of her own involvement in it all. When she was silent like this, Tsitsi couldn't help but think of the title of one of her favourite books, Kunyayara Hakusi Kutaura? She had never asked for Tsitsi's help, but now that she knew she didn't have the luxury to refuse the money, she kept her words to herself, recognising her complicity. Tsitsi strained as she felt the effort of her self-control.

Mama had remained quiet throughout the roora negotiations between the uncles in both Zvobgo's and Babamukuru Edzai's delegations. This allowed them to use her house and she performed the duties required of her, but she had shown her displeasure in a way that most hurt Tsitsi. She simply withdrew from her daughter. Tsitsi was not used to being angry with her mother, but a hot energy flowed through her now, causing her to barely contain herself. Her temples were throbbing.

Usually, thoughts of her mother's sacrifices could pacify any incipient anger and push it back down into her belly, her instinct to tie a cloth tight across it to secure the fire from escaping and burning any bridges between them, but this time she felt increasingly annoyed that she was being held ransom by them. At least she was grateful, appreciative of her mother's sacrifices.

Sacrifice!

Sacrifice!

Sacrifice!

Tsitsi's left hand slid from the couch and inadvertently hit the wood of the armrest.

The dull thud alerted Mama and Sekuru's eyes to her. She clenched her left fist as she briefly closed her eyes. In an attempt to discharge her anger to a more useful purpose, she got up to direct Susan in the adjacent kitchen, unpacking the boxes Tsitsi had brought.

Decisively, she took a box from Susan's hands, placed it on top of the wooden cupboard and began unpacking its contents of jam, yoghurt, biscuits and all the other sweet things her mother had never taken a liking to, but that Zvobgo had insisted on. Tsitsi took some of these and placed them in an emptied box for Susan to take home. Then she reasoned that giving Susan jam, yoghurt and biscuits was impractical. Hupfu, cooking oil, salt and other basics would be more useful to Susan, so she settled on unpacking two more boxes and placing them in the box destined for Susan.

Not trusting her uncle to resist the temptation to sell the items instead of giving them to Susan, she gestured to the boxes, "O, Susan. Take this to your brothers and sisters kumusha."

Susan's eyes widened, but she quickly restrained herself from kneeling and other shows of gratitude, gestures that she knew Tsitsi despised. She confined her gratitude to clapping her cupped hands, "Mazvita Mama, tatenda."

Tsitsi nodded, and now somewhat cooled by Susan's show of gratitude, she focused her attention on the fridge

Zvobgo had bought as a gift as part of the roora negotiations. She pulled the door open. There was no hum and no light came on. She was ready to launch into a tirade for Susan not telling her that the fridge wasn't working so that she could have had it fixed or replaced, but then remembered that there was load shedding on that side of town. She quickly found another fault.

"Nhai, Susan, why are we struggling for lights here? Why don't you put on the generator? We don't buy these things for nothing. That's the job of a generator. To generate electricity."

The girl responded meekly, "Mama, I didn't want the diesel to get finished quickly."

"Who told you to worry about that? If it finishes, then it finishes! We will buy more. That is the job of money – to buy things! To provide for our needs. Let me be the one to worry about that."

Susan cowered: "Horaiti, Mama, I will tell you next time."

Tsitsi peered into the fridge and shook her head when she saw the rotting vegetables for which Mama and Sekuru had no use. She had warned Zvobgo that the food from Bon Marche would be competing with the food from the Mbare Market for a place on their plates. And of course, Mbare's finest had won, leaving the likes of mushrooms and baby marrows to go bad.

The glass bottles of cooldrink and water, and the plastic cups of yoghurt were sweating. The one indulgence that Mama had allowed herself was a childlike desire for hard-to-source banana yoghurt.

She closed the door, grateful that her mother's ageing had been limited to that. That her mother had not, unlike other people her age, begun to descend into a second infancy – she was too fit for that.

Once Susan had left the kitchen to turn on the generator outside, she walked to the stove and removed the pot's lid. To her delight there was boiled chibage. She picked a cob from the pot and pulled out a kitchen chair to eat it, remembering how Mama would pinch her ear, and then warn that if she continued with this impatient behaviour of hers, it would rain down in sheets on her wedding day. In those days as a child, her hunger was too immediate for such foresight. Now as a grown woman she would be more than grateful for a rain-filled white wedding day, as long as she had the white wedding.

With a cooler head, she returned to the sitting room. They watched the credits of the Chinese film before she decided to leave.

"Mama, I'm going now. Zvakanakai."

As she rose from her seat, Mama spoke, her voice faint from disuse, "Before you leave, let us pray."

2

Tsitsi and Zvobgo had seated themselves at each end of the dining table. Wrapped up in her own meandering thoughts, she was startled when Kasongo, Zvobgo's Congolese bodyguard, and Robson, the cook, entered the room. She was still ill at ease with the idea that her newfound status as Zvobgo's partner came with people as accessories. Nor was she comfortable with the idea of them as gatekeepers with access to the details of their personal lives.

Whenever she felt herself shrinking under the indifferent glare of the staff that surrounded her, as she did in this instance, she would straighten her back and lift her chin in the way that her trusted Chiedza had instructed her.

She did not like the lack of expression of the house staff. They had a brusque, efficient manner about them, but made no further pretence. She imagined that they resented her, and that that resentment had grown in intensity from secret ridicule and disdain to open resistance.

Initially, she approximated the Magnanimous Madam,

going out of her way to greet and enquire ("Makadii Sekuru? Masiya vamwe kumusha vari sei? Mbuya vakazopona here?", "Manheru Sisi, maswera sei?") and to show gratitude ("Maita basa Sekuru!"; "Eii, mufunge, mandibatsira sterek, Sisi!"). But she had soon stopped, switching instead to the cold English of the greeting with no enquiry ("Good morning;" "Good afternoon;" "Good evening.") and gratitude that was no longer gratuitous ("Thank you."). She was sure that her familiarity was breeding contempt—and not only in response to her over-friendliness, but because of their shared origins.

She imagined, too, that they sometimes spat in her food. There was not enough deference in them to shake the unsettling sense that her position was a precarious one. The way they looked at her had a directness that felt insolent and accusatory. It felt mocking, as if they were just waiting for her to slip and show her Strong Rural Background (SRB), something she had been self-conscious of since boarding school. Her classmates, including Takura and his crew, had seized on the fact she was not a Born-Location like them and had only moved to Harare after Form 1. Having their own trunks full of tuck, they would laugh at the way she and the other SRBs scrambled for pieces of makoko to later slather with margarine when the cooks would scrape out the remaining pieces of sadza from the bottom of their big pots. Having always had electricity, they would laugh and ask Tsitsi and the other SRBs if their eyes were coping with having lights for the first time.

And now, whenever the house staff in Zvobgo's home were behind her, she would turn quickly to face them. She was sure that if she gave them enough time they would almost certainly mime mockingly, "Imagine! Not even a

Born-Location, but she is acting like munhu we Nose Brigade!" Yes, she was sure that one day they would trip her up and all her Strong Rural Background-ness, and the State Registered Baranzi-ness that she was sure they attached to her, would spill out from behind the tightly held façade like rubbish out of a too-small refuse bag.

She pursed her lips at the memory of when Elijah, one of the kitchen boys, had come to her, shy and timid, asking for bus fare. She had shouted back at him, "I am not your relative! Don't ask me for such things!"

She felt it had taken something away from her, this audacity to even ask her, as if they were from the same village or something.

As Chiedza had advised, all she could do was continue with her authority as Madam, until she felt that all who worked for her knew and respected that she was the new Woman of the House and no longer the Small House.

With a metal dish in Kasongo's left hand, the dish towel in readiness over his left forearm and a jug filled with hot, soapy water in his other, the routine began: Kasongo handed the jug over to Robson, who poured the water over Zvobgo's big hands, Zvobgo washed his hands, Robson moved back, Kasongo stepped forward, Kasongo offered the drying towel and Zvobgo dried his hands.

"Did you take the groceries to Mama?" Zvobgo asked Tsitsi.

"I did," she hesitated as she thought about her visit to her seemingly indifferent mother and added, "She was very grateful. She sends her thanks."

Robson made his way over to Tsitsi at the opposite end of the table. Robson poured the water over Tsitsi's delicate hands, Tsitsi washed her hands, Robson moved back,

Kasongo stepped forward, Kasongo offered the towel and Tsitsi dried her hands.

The two men retreated to the kitchen.

"You know, it's not safe for an old woman to be living alone in the location, or anywhere else for that matter. Have you told her that she is welcome to move in here?"

"She's not alone. She has Sekuru Dickson," Tsitsi paused, contemplating the idea of her old uncle acting as protector of his even older sister, "and there is Susan, the house girl. Mama is not alone; they are both there to look after her."

Kasongo and Robson reappeared with the food. Like disenchanted cupbearers, they placed the plates in front of Zvobgo and Tsitsi, alongside the superfluous silverware. Superfluous because Zvobgo insisted on being served only traditional meals to be eaten by hand, because he did not have, as he put it, a 'colonised palate.' He also insisted that traditional meals prevented the need—as harboured by many of his peers—for various pills and tablets, to lower blood pressure, raise iron levels, lower cholesterol, ease the passage of blood through his veins to his heart and whatever else that needed to be lowered, raised or eased.

Tsitsi, though, was suspicious of the rationales proffered by Zvobgo. She suspected that it was more an attempt on his part to accommodate her perceived 'ruralness.' She felt insulted. Zvobgo knew that she had gone to one of the best mission boarding schools in the country; the kind where the boarding masters and mistresses insisted that the students learn table etiquette. Of course, she was perfectly at ease with a knife and fork. For the first few months she had insisted on using the silverware at every meal, even for sadza, but as she saw that Zvobgo remained unrelenting in his insistence on traditional food, she eventually resigned herself to using her hands.

"Your uncle can move in too. I just don't like the idea of an old person looking after another old person," he paused, "and that house girl is too young. You rely on her too much. People your mother's age need continuity." Ironic words, Tsitsi thought to herself, for Zvobgo was not even her mother's age mate; he was significantly older. "Soon that girl will be married off and that will be the last you hear of her. You know these people."

Married—something they were not. Tsitsi bristled at the word and immediately fell silent. How could he speak about it so casually, even mention it when he knew it remained a thorn in her flesh? This was the very reason her mother would not give her approval of the liaison and, in so doing, ratify the relationship in Tsitsi's conscience. She suppressed the resentment she could feel itching up; she dared not bring up the question of marriage herself. Marriage is something to be initiated by the man. It would happen when he was ready. Even Chiedza agreed with this.

"The food is getting cold," she said, although it was steaming with thick vapour. She bowed her head and offered her palms to Zvobgo, "Let us pray."

Zvobgo was only nominally observant, but nonetheless, he indulged Tsitsi in the ritual and he too bowed his head and clasped his hands in prayer.

Sign of the Cross.

"Bless us, O Lord, and these Thy gifts, which we are about to receive from Thy bounty, through Christ our Lord. Amen."

Sign of the Cross.

Zvobgo raised his head and nodded to signal that Kasongo and Robson could resume. Robson began by tasting a morsel of each contingent of the meal on Zvobgo's plate: first the sadza (to be sure, sadza rezviyo, because Zvobgo thought it the healthiest kind), then the nyama, and finally the muriwo. After the last swallow, the cook stuck his tongue out and then stepped back to allow Kasongo to do the same. Kasongo ate, then swallowed and stuck his tongue out. Satisfied that neither keeled over dead, Zvobgo instructed they do the same for Tsitsi's meal.

Tsitsi's bowels began to move and her stomach gave an embarrassing grumble. Many times she had been tempted to point out that it was unnecessary to have both Kasongo and Robson tasting both meals separately when they could do it simultaneously. They could even alternate the plates on a random basis.

Instead she sat quietly, waiting, as Zvobgo pinched the sadza between his thick fingers. He blew his breath onto the soft brown mound before placing it in his mouth. She tried not to follow his movements too carefully and attempted to distract herself by tracing the outlines of the green-and-brown patches of Kasongo's uniform or the details of the white burglar bars that obscured the view of Mrs Zvobgo's rose garden illuminated by floodlights or the intricate embroidery that patterned the curtains Mrs Zvobgo had designed when she had redecorated the place two years before.

But even as she busied her eyes with the room's details, her ears did not escape the mxm-mxm of Zvobgo's masticating teeth as he chewed the sadza and muriwo into what she imagined as a greenish-brown mess. She also knew when he began with the meat, as she heard his teeth working harder to tear at the sinews of the flesh.

To show his satisfaction, Zvobgo nodded and—as if the nod broke the string that held their lungs closed—Robson and Kasongo, who had been watching anxiously, released their bated breath and breathed freely. Tsitsi could now begin her own meal.

Before Zvobgo resumed talk of her mother, she distracted him by talking about his recent listening tour with so-called people on the ground. He responded as expected.

"This is the government of our people's own making. Every fellow countryman is a brother for whom we are building the nation. Why would anyone want to be against that? He has such vaporous ideology. It is everything and nothing—no intellectual underpinning whatsoever."

Tsitsi listened carefully as Zvobgo shook his head and waved his hand dismissively, almost connecting with Robson who had leaned in to pour some water. Her silence was punctuated with mhhmms, oh?s, requests for Zvobgo to re-explain the structures of the politburo, and intermittent shows of humble awe at his explanations of complex matters. He in turn enjoyed this and diligently schooled this pleasant girl.

THE BEDROOM WAS LARGE, kept spacious by the minimalist furniture Mrs Zvobgo had chosen and that Tsitsi had not dared change. During the day, the room felt airy, the light penetrating her cream linen curtains. There was always the scent of flowers in the air, as they were brought in from the garden designed by and arranged daily as per Mrs Zvobgo's original instructions.

Initially, Tsitsi had not dared disrupt any of this domestic order. It had been a welcome diversion from the dingy edge-of-town hotel she and Zvobgo had patronised before Mrs Zvobgo finally packed up and left. But as Tsitsi began to settle in, that order began to feel like a deliberate orchestration by Mrs Zvobgo's shadow, intended to taunt the interloper and her less-than-urbane ways. Many times Tsitsi was tempted to order a redecoration, but where to begin? What if she produced something garish and howlingly gaudy? She was sure that even the house staff would see any efforts on her part inferior to Mrs Zvobgo's.

For a while, the memory of her and Zvobgo's hotel haunts kept Tsitsi uncomplaining.

She had been clumsy at first. Even after countless consultations with Chiedza, which included watching old porn DVDs, her nerves had ensured that she forgot to caress and stroke, rather than grope and grab. Many times she could not keep her hand steady, she was so nervous. His erection seemed to haunt her in the way that it intimated Fata Masika's knobkerrie. She imagined being chastised by him. She was having sex before marriage, destroying her temple, sacrificing her virtue. But, as she trembled and swallowed the knobkerrie, she disconnected herself, reminding herself that she needed to eat and, with time and Chiedza's encouragement, she learnt to engross herself wholly in the act.

Zvobgo in the meantime was patient. As she began to improve her technique, he began to open up, tell Tsitsi about Mrs Zvobgo. That Mrs Zvobgo did not support him. That she wanted to move and make a 'fresh start.' That she did not understand that it was in his destiny to lead. That Mrs Zvobgo was too stubborn. That she was too self-righteous. That she did not even want to touch him.

It was then that Tsitsi began to feel uncomfortable in the hotel room. That it was small was not a problem, for the bedsitter flat she rented in Avenues was hardly much bigger. It was rather that she had been brought up believing, as her mother and boarding mistress had instilled in her, "Cleanliness is next to Godliness." She began to feel the dirtiness of the room: that the sheets had stains and looked like they had last seen water in the days of Smith; that the carpet smelt of mildew, last replaced in the times of the Chief Harare; that the room's sink was discoloured from the constant drip of a leaky tap; that the hotel was in a dingy part of town, one that she would ordinarily have avoided; that there was a homeless man who pushed his way through the equally bothersome forex dealers to greet Tsitsi and Zvobgo whenever they entered the hotel lobby, where inevitably the real prostitutes would make themselves at home, bums and breasts spilling out of their clothes.

But all of that was a distant memory now, as she lay in the comfort of their king-sized bed, her moist walls receiving him as he entered her slowly.

3

Just as it had been for Mama, school and church had been the axes of Tsitsi's existence. The goals impressed on her were sanctity and scholastic achievement. If she was not being admonished for not knowing that it was John Smith Moffat who had established the first permanent mission in Matabeleland, she was being reprimanded for forgetting that the Book of Leviticus came after Exodus and not Deuteronomy.

"Cleanliness is next to Godliness, and Learnedness is next to Cleanliness," was the frequent refrain in her mother's house where every night the family service was held and, without fail, was followed by closely monitored studying.

Silent prayer and determined reading. Silent prayer and determined reading. Silent prayer and determined reading. That was her life.

On mass days, Fata Masika would enter the church, signalling the beginning of the service. The choir members would make their way up the aisles from the back of the church, singing in a serious, solemn tone, only lifting their eyes from their hymnals to gaze ahead to the altar where Fata Masika stood. As they walked, they took on new affectations, distancing themselves from their everyday identities and the rest of the congregation.

Unlike the mass that was accompanied by drums and even dancing at Holy Trinity, there was no instrumental accompaniment to the singing in Fata Masika's chapel. The melodies were slow, mournful, fitting with the life of austerity and service to God that Fata Masika called for. Its solemnity was meant to summon calm introspection, but for most of the children in attendance it only summoned a sense of impatience as they suffered through the hour-long service, a drag that came as a life sentence.

Fata Masika's movements were so slight and solemn as to be ceremonial. He spoke softly, without the variance and volume that often came with a preacher's voice in sermon. They sometimes strained to hear him.

At school they learnt by rote. In fact, the approach was so effective that up until now, even in Zvobgo's bed, she could readily reproduce their Ghanaian English teacher Mr Sunday's dictations line by line. On occasion, he would also give impromptu history lessons: "In 1965, Ian Douglas Smith declared Independence from Britain." In 1965 Ian Douglas Smith declared Independence from Britain. "In 1888, King Lobengula granted the Rudd Concession to Cecil John Rhodes." In 1888 King Lobengula granted the Rudd Concession to Cecil John Rhodes. "In 1885, Sir David Livingstone discovered Victoria Falls." In 1885, Sir David Livingstone discovered Victoria Falls. "Great Zimbabwe was built by the Mutapa Dynasty, which thrived from the eleventh to the fourteenth century." Great Zimbabwe was built by the Mutapa Dynasty, which thrived from the eleventh to the fourteenth century.

Although Tsitsi loved maths and dreamt of becoming a banker—a Reserve Bank governor, in fact—English remained her favourite subject. Not so much because she loved the language, but because Mr Sunday, their English teacher, was a welcome relief from the world of routine and repetition.

In a mission school that had inherited the European doctrine of curing children of their superstitions by any means necessary, Mr Sunday stood out. It was the nineties, and yet he sported a Patrice Lumumba-esque side parting. In one of the many impromptu history lessons he gave, he told the story of the brave African martyr, Thomas Sankara. From then on the class called him Sankara—and he took a liking to it. He'd had an almost fetish-like obsession with the 'native condition.' He took pleasure in poking and probing, causing discomfort with the many safely established beliefs upheld by the school.

One day the class was reading Things Fall Apart.

Sankara had asked Takura Kanyangarara to read an excerpt aloud. He read how, with a heavy heart, Okonkwo had just executed the Oracle's decree that he kill Ikemefuna, the boy the village had received as reparation for the murder of one of their women, and had by then called Okonkwo 'Father' for the time he had spent in his household and the relationship they had developed.

"How barbaric!" the class shouted in unison.

"But, Teacher, how could people be so senseless?" Takura pleaded in disbelief.

Sankara smiled. "Ah, but, Takura, those people are just as senseless as you Christians."

Some of the class's resident geniuses jolted up, indignant, and started laughing, "How can you compare us to them, Sankara?"

"Well, did Abraham not prepare his darling son Isaac to be sacrificed because his God had asked him to do so for no apparent reason? Were you not learning this as one of the greatest acts of faith displayed by one of God's sons?"

"Yes, Sankara, but the difference is that God exists. His word and His commandments are right, sir, even when we do not understand."

"So then, Takura, tell me, what is so different when it comes to Okonkwo? Neither Abraham nor Okonkwo could give physical evidence of their god or gods existing? They were both acting in faith, were they not?"

This little lesson from Sankara had tickled Tsitsi, not so much for the near-blasphemous comparison, but for the fact that Sankara had shown up her rival. It in fact tickled her so much that she repeated it that night in the dorm room during their study period. Her boarding mistress, Miss Matsamba, caught wind of it and summoned Tsitsi to the entrance of their dorm room.

The room grew tense. They knew that Miss Matsamba was not like the other teachers who were partial to giving manual labour of the distasteful kind, such as hoeing the garden of vegetables or cleaning the toilets for a week as punishment for bad behaviour. They knew that, even though it had long been outlawed, she had no qualms about using corporal punishment and that none of them would dare complain.

Sternly, and with the eyes of all the boarding girls on her, she impatiently gestured for Tsitsi to turn and face the wall.

Tsitsi didn't need to be told to bend over. She soon felt

the fall of the cane, striking her haunches and then the backs of her legs. She was grateful it was not on her bum; it would take some days for the welts to go down, so at least she could sit somewhat painlessly if she remained on the edge of the seat, which in any case kept her posture upright and would prevent further corporal punishment from the other teachers, especially Mr Muchemwa, for slouchiness.

She was numb at first and almost wanted to strut back to her chair in a nonchalant manner, proud that she had been able to endure the blows without any tears and without even feeling any pain. But that was short-lived, because just as quickly as the thought had come to her, she felt a hot stinging sensation shoot through her, as the skin that had been impacted raised itself into welts that looked like fat worms. Her eyes immediately filled with tears and could no longer delay her scream, her plea for her mother.

Tears dropped from Tsitsi's eyes, because, although Mama had never laid a hand on her, her desire for her daughter to do well meant that she had a high tolerance for corporal punishment, even though it was not entirely legal, so the child knew it would be futile seeking her mother's sympathy for this.

4

Her books had never been able to lift her to the heights that the Old Testament did, but nonetheless she found herself immersed in them. She worked diligently each weeknight and on weekends too. It was as if Mama was always there with her, lodged firmly in her mind like a silent cheerleader prodding her on.

Often she would work all through the night. She would study in the dining hall and then right up until it was lights out. Then she'd wait until she was sure the senior prefects and matron were sleeping before she would go into the corridor and sit with her blanket wrapped around her as she read by the corridor light.

The interesting studying habits she adopted before tests became even more peculiar with exams. This included keeping a textbook under her pillow and, like an evening and morning prayer, she recited the periodic table, important historical dates, Pythagorean theory and whatever other texts were relevant to the applicable subject before she slept and as soon as she woke up. This earned her the nickname

'Osmosis' from her dorm mates, because it seemed that that was in effect when she took the top position in class each term. While studying at a desk, her feet would rest in a basin or bucket of cold water. In a book on Winston Churchill, she had read of his micro-napping habits, which allowed him to survive on four hours' sleep a night. Or something to that effect. She tried it, but the exercise had ended abruptly with lashings from Miss Matsamba after she fell asleep during study period.

Later, at university, she would be introduced to caffeine pills, which she eventually refrained from, when they caused a bout of depression during her second-year final exams.

Takura was said not to study at all. Indeed, as many of his dorm mates would confirm, when they were up all night studying, he was sound asleep. He had even started his own club, which convened religiously every afternoon. It was known as the AFCFL – Advocates For A Care-Free Life.

As the leader, Takura would tell them that all he had to do was eat eggs before the exams and that was it! Tsitsi subscribed to this egg theory, but only as a complement to her preparation. Another favourite schoolteacher, Mrs Chimombe, who taught science, had confirmed this, saying that eggs were good for the brain. So, during her exam period, Tsitsi studied through the night by light of the bulb, paraffin lamp or candle, feet submerged in water, and ate as many boiled eggs as she could afford to bribe the cooks to boil for her in an effort to build up stores of intelligence that would be discharged as she wrote her exams.

Takura would sit on the veranda of the boys' boarding house, the one flanked on each side by flowerbeds bordered with red bricks buried diagonally, scraping the sinewy flesh of a mango with his teeth, and sell his theory to those eager to imitate his scholastic success.

"Tsitsi's nose is always in books. She only gets high marks because she kills herself studying. Have you ever seen her without a book?" he once laughed smugly.

"What do you mean, Takura? How else do you do well?" she protested.

He ignored her and continued.

"Otherwise she's just a dunderhead. Who else can study like that? Only someone who knows they are really not clever and must punish themselves. I don't blame her. Not everyone can have the natural intelligence I have."

In a huff she left, and sheepishly opened her books to begin studying furiously like the dunderhead Takura claimed she was.

Tsitsi had eventually begun to believe Takura's claims that she was really a dunderhead until one day, early on in the term, she had spotted him paging furiously through his schoolbooks, studying when all the others were doing the weekly groundwork. How he had got away with missing the compulsory groundwork was a mystery to her. She resisted the urge to shout that he was a liar and that he was the real dunderhead between the two of them. Instead, she returned to her books, and studied as diligently as ever, smiling smugly at him whenever he began with his 'retort.' Of course she beat him in the exams that followed, and that was enough, leaving her feeling no need to expose him to the boarding masters for his game of truancy.

Not unsurprisingly, as the years went on, Takura remained dismissive of her as they took turns taking first place in class. When he would beat her, he would attribute it to her weakness as a girl. When she overtook him, he would call it luck. And when it became consecutive first places, and his friends had no choice but to acknowledge her brainy prowess by proclaiming, "Anodya maB!", Takura would respond, "Muroyi!", repeatedly denouncing her and declaring her witchcraft to all who would listen.

5

As the students waited for their economics lecturer to appear on the first day of classes, a girl stood up in front of the lecture hall acting the fool. The girl was not particularly beautiful but she made an effort and took care of herself and, to the annoyance of men and women alike, was also strikingly aware of her effect on men.

Unlike Tsitsi, who was inattentive to her appearance, using her intellect and focus on books as an excuse, this girl clearly took every care in making sure she was more than just presentable. It was this girl who would later teach Tsitsi to shave her bushy eyebrows and replace them by a delicately arched pencil. It was this harlot who taught her to relax, curl and even dye her own hair in the dorm room they shared, to paint her nails without making a mess, to line her lips so that the lipstick would not 'bleed.'

On that first day, it was Chiedza who had been performing in front of the chalkboard for the benefit of the class. Chiedza, soon to become Tsitsi's best friend. Chiedza, the organiser of dances and other social activities for the Student Representative Council. Tsitsi, on the other hand, a member in good standing of the Students' Christian Organisation. It was perhaps to be expected that the two would become friends—they were the only girls in that economics class. The economics department was one where Tsitsi and Chiedza had played the wrong roles. Here, the women were administrators, and the men, the students and academic staff.

Despite this, Chiedza began in her best professor's voice: "Dearest scholars of economics! The erudite class of 2004! Well, that is if all of you can manage to make it that far! Some of you might be taken by crocodiles in the Limpopo as you border-jump to South Africa! Some of you might be Central Intelligence Officers who remain in First Year for the next ten years! Some of you might just be dunderheads who should have tried the likes of Africa University or Solusi or even that new women's university that I hear will be opening soon!"

As was expected, her arrogant, almost-all-male-but-for-one classmates laughed harder at her university elitism than her Central Intelligence joke.

"Now," she turned her body to the chalkboard and began furiously drawing the axes of a graph, "the first principle that you must make yourselves familiar with, as the erudite economics scholars of 2004, is that of ceteris pari—"

"Eh, excuse me, 'Professor Nhingi,'" one boy, Tashinga, stood up and interrupted her and went on to quote one of the many books he had read in anticipation of the course, saying, "It is said that 'marriage is often the surest way out of poverty for many poorer women.' Indeed, the best chance they have is good grooming! Saka inzwaika sistren, you can just carry on concerning yourself nezve make-up nemagogo enyu. Leave the graphs to us who can understand and put them to good use."

But instead of an embarrassed silence, this sistren would have none of it.

"I'm sure the same thing can be said for you boys who will soon become the bitches of ministers who follow the way of banana."

There was a stunned hush as the class was shocked by the crudeness that came from the girl's perfectly lined lips. Before they could jump in with even cruder comebacks, Professor Makumbe walked into the lecture hall with the exaggerated affectations expected of one who is multiple-degreed. He stood in front of the class, textbook in hand, as the boys muttered under their breath, upset that they hadn't had the opportunity to deliver the comebacks they were sure would put this Chiedza in her place.

Even in her shyness, Tsitsi scoffed at Tashinga's condescension. While she would rather not have agreed with what Chiedza had said about ministers being like banana— and so reinforce the attitudes of these young men—Tsitsi wished she too had had that kind of confidence. As it turned out, it was the same confidence that allowed Chiedza to make regular contributions to class discussions and arguments. The rest of the class, the men, were initially surprised that she knew enough—and had the self-assurance —to say something. This was especially true when she knew Chiedza had the balls, or, as Chiedza said, the vagina to contradict them. In time, the surprise wore off and became something of an expectation that would find them actually asking whether she had anything to add. This was the expectation that provided the confidence Tsitsi herself needed to make contributions and contradictions of her own.

As if picking up from where Chiedza had left off, Professor Makumbe began: "Welcome to the world of ceteris paribus. All things being equal, if things continue the way they are, this basic economic concept—the foundation of all functional economies—will become increasingly abstract for you, you poor students of this generation."

Over the next few years, Tsitsi found herself fully immersed in the model world of ceteris paribus. All things being equal. All things remaining the same. A world where if this, then that, if y then x, ruled. A world where, if there are shorter labour hours then, ceteris paribus, the volume of output will decrease. Where if there are more labour hours then, ceteris paribus, the volume of output will increase. A world where the greater the effort exerted then, ceteris paribus, the greater the success. An increasingly useless paradigm where the reality it sought to explain was far from the same.

There was always talk during lectures, in between lectures, in between mouthfuls in the dining hall, in between the cafeteria queues, in between passengers in the kombi on the way home between varsity and Kuwadzana during school holidays. All had become pundits and analysts.

It was better if it was stagnant. Instead it was free falling. The food scarcity. The petrol shortage. The drought.

Sure, Tsitsi had experienced the chaos, but somehow living in her abstract world where the principle of ceteris paribus dominated, she managed to ignore most of these conversations until she exited the gates of campus and made the transition to labourer, where hours, output and income were supposed to be measured in a model world of ceteris paribus, but instead seemed to be calculated according to the rules of jambanja.

6

"Ko, Tsitsi? What's going on with this get-up of yours?"

Chiedza picked at a fold in Tsitsi's towering violent-pink head wrap.

"Please, ChiChi, it's a gele. It's what Rita Dominic and Genevieve Nnaji are always wearing."

"Vakakunyepera! It's called a sweet wrapper!" Chiedza was barely able to contain a laugh as she led Tsitsi into the small sitting room.

"People need to see me as a respectable wife to Zvobgo. I'm tired of being confused for that daughter of his! His people keep saying to me ..." she put on a nasal voice, "'Oh! We didn't know that you'd be back so soon! How was Malaysia? How is your mother?'"

"All right then," Chiedza gave her a look as if to question her continued pretence to decency when she had already foregone so much else, but it quickly disappeared and melted with her happiness at seeing Tsitsi. "What are you so worried about? He paid roora for you, didn't he? Ten heads of cattle and yet you are still insecure about this? Is it because he hasn't made it official in the eyes of God?"

"I am worried. I mean, no, I'm not worried. That's just a formality. I'm his traditional wife. It's just that I can't be running around in mini-skirts like you. I live in the Main House. I am not a Small House."

"Uri kutii Tsitsi? Are you saying that I am a Small House?"

She clapped her hands and feigned the indignation of the scorned woman of the many Nollywood movies they had watched together during study breaks at university. "God forbid-o! How can you say such a thing? An abomination! I am not a Small House!" She clapped her hands again, "Hey! I am not a Small House-o! I will take that gele of yours!" To emphasise her point, she sucked on her tongue, feigning even more indignation. "Mxm!"

She leapt forward, raising her hand as if to decrown Tsitsi, but stopped as she collapsed into laughter, causing them both to tumble onto Chiedza's bed.

They lay on top of each other for a while before Tsitsi grew pensive.

"Ko, why so serious?"

Tsitsi waved her hand absentmindedly to dismiss her silence as nothing. Never one to tolerate silence, Chiedza chimed in, "I can't decide, who looks better between you and the Oga's wife? You look like you've stolen one of her outfits!"

Tsitsi played along, sucking a "Mxm! Abomination!" as she clapped her hands. "I, me, Tsitsi, cannot be compared to this woman-o! Hey! Look at this fabric-o!"

She held out a swathe of the Vlisco cloth for Chiedza to touch, and she indeed obliged.

"Hmm, you are right. I am sorry, my sista-o, there is no comparison."

Chiedza saw that Tsitsi's frown had finally relaxed into a smile and took her hand. "Hesi shaaz. How are you, my dear? You've been hiding since you moved to Highlands. Am I not good enough for you to visit any more?"

"Mushe, I can't complain too much," she shrugged. "I'm just doing what I can."

"You mean to tell me that even as Zvobgo's woman uri kukiya kiya like the rest of us?"

"Aiwa, ChiChi, don't be silly. I'm not hustling anything," Tsitsi paused and drew in a breath. "I'm okay, except for this thing that Sekuru dared to show me."

She pulled out the crumpled flier and handed it to Chiedza, whose eyes she carefully watched as they flitted over the list and grew wide as they found themselves lower on the page.

Unable to wait for her to finish, Tsitsi anticipated her reaction, "Have you ever seen such a thing?"

Chiedza remained silent, still studying the paper. Finally she looked up and gripped Tsitsi, who by now was on the edge of the seat. "I can't believe this! It's terrible!"

"Just imagine! What was I supposed to do with it?"

Chiedza paused, then shook her head and spoke in a grave, measured voice. "Such terrible, terrible ..."—her eyes widened—"... spelling and grammar!"

Tsitsi flung her head back, incredulous at Chiedza's irreverence. "Mxm! Chiedza, if you're just going to make a joke of me, then I'd better go!"

She rose, picking up her bag, but Chiedza quickly grabbed her arm and pulled her back down into her seat.

"Sorry, T. No more jokes, okay?" She picked up the paper again. "What did you say to him after you read it?"

"Ndaiti chiiko, Chiedza? He's my uncle! But I was so angry, sha. I could only say that Mama wouldn't be happy with such things. I wanted to say more, of course. I wanted to tell him how wrong it is. The witchdoctor, the sex. Imagine, Chiedza! What's the meaning of this?"

"You could maybe say something about the witchcraft, but, Tsitsi, how could you want to say anything to your mother's brother about sex when you are living in sin with Zvobgo?"

"Chiedza! Hatisi kuchaya mapoto!"

"Don't blame me for the truth—you are the one who is a devout Catholic girl who doesn't value her traditional marriage. According to that logic, you are living in sin. Not too far from Sekuru's actions."

"Argh, you can't compare us. Mine is not for any enjoyment. You know the situation."

"Business and pleasure?"

"Don't be so vulgar, Chiedza! What situation does Sekuru have, in any case? I do everything for him. No bread queues for him. Zvobgo brings him so much bread he could wipe his hands with it. He doesn't have to worry his old mind about prices or forex rates—the money just comes to him, already converted! When his brothers are kumusha eating that USAID bulgur wheat, he is eating corn flakes in town! And if he is tired of corn flakes and life in town and he wants to go kumusha to go and plant, he can do it. Zvobgo will send more fertiliser than he even has the land for! And he would surely organise a tractor for him too! So, tell me, Chiedza, why does he need the help of this fly-by-night? Not even a real healer! Is that how desperate he is? Really, what more does he want?"

"Ah, T, you know that's just the hunger of the stomach that you are feeding. You won't satisfy the hunger of his loins," Chiedza shrugged. "You know how men are. Mbuya wangu used to say, 'Murume imbwa,' a man is a man is a dog. Whether he is your husband, your boyfriend, your brother, your father, your uncle—a man is a dog. That's life, what can we do?"

Chiedza reached for her arm.

"Come now, Tsitsi, you're too young to die of high blood pressure. Relax. You and I both know that the best thing is just to get on with what you need to do and try not to think too much about these things. Handitika?"

Tsitsi heaved a heavy sigh as Chiedza moved a hand to her shoulder and finally smiled. "Anyway, Chi, how are you?"

Chiedza shrugged. "Ah, ndingati kudii? Marie, Jan and the rest are going back to the Netherlands, so it looks like we'll have to shut down the NGO."

"I'm sure there must be other NGOs looking for locals?"

"You know that your husband and his crew are clamping down on NGOs—we won't be the only ones closing. But, it's not a problem. I'm using some of the dollars I've saved as starting capital, so I'll call my friend Ruvhi at the bank and we'll find a way to burn it on the black market. In the meantime, I'll get pocket money from my ministers of finance."

She laughed an infectious laugh that Tsitsi caught unwillingly. She shook her head, "Sahwira vangu, always scheming. Last time he told me he was going to kuSouth to buy eggs and then resell them here."

"And how did that go?"

"Ah, that old man," she laughed, "imagine him trying to keep up with vakadzi vemadoily on those Tenda buses eku South."

"I'm sure he was a hard worker in his day. You can't expect him to just sit down now. It's not like what you have, where you can lie on your back, think of the Great Zimbabwe and all will come to you."

Tsitsi immediately withdrew again. She was always painfully aware of how her relationship with Zvobgo could be perceived. But, she sometimes wondered, how much of what they perceived could she claim was really far from the truth.

"For all my comments, Tsitsi, I think what you have is the best kind of arrangement. I really envy it."

"What do you mean?"

"Well, my theory is that the most successful relationships are ones where the expectations are clear. You know very well that Zvobgo must never come home to find you wearing tracksuits and a dhuku. Ivo, vaZvobgo vanoziva damn well that you must never come to a situation where there is not ample food in the kitchen, ZESA in the house or fuel in the car. Easy. No room for confusion."

"You and your theories, Chiedza! That doesn't even describe us—me and Zvobgo," Tsitsi smarted at the cold description. "I'm a companion to Zvobgo. He confides in me and I listen to him. I respect what he has to say. That's much more than I can say for Mrs Zvobgo, who could only find ways to dismiss him and undermine him in front of people."

"However you want to see it, Tsitsi, the bottom line is that the expectations for what needs to be done to keep either party happy are clear. It's not like you are also asking for him to be some sort of Romeo. He is there to provide. And he is not asking you to listen and be an intellectual equal. The fundamentals are clear. Hapana kurasika."

"Fundamentals? Fundamentals? You might as well say the fundamentals of sex!" But before she launched into another justification for her relationship, she stopped and narrowed her eyes at Chiedza. "Chiedza, why am I always defending this relationship to you? What kind of a friend are you when you are judgemental?"

I have enough of it from myself, she wanted to say.

"Hey! Don't talk with that tone now. Who else can you speak to about Zvobgo?" Chiedza spoke with her faux-Nigerian accent before switching back to her own voice. "My dear, if I was really interested in judging you, I would have gone and done it in the streets, gossiping about you and Zvobgo like the rest of that office. I am your sister — unozviziva—and all you will get from me is honesty. But, I want you to be honest with yourself too. With all of this chaos around us and the funny choices we have to make because of it, it's the only way to stay sane. Otherwise, I'll be the one who has to book you into eHlanyeni."

Having diffused the situation once again, Chiedza quickly changed the subject.

"Look at me! I'm so rude! I haven't offered you anything to eat. You're going to tell everyone that I'm stingy. Let me cook now before the electricity goes off." She got up and mimicked the voice of the church gossip guest reporting findings to an outsider: "Chiedza haaite! Anonyima chikafu!"

"Don't worry, Chiedza. It's getting late, I'm sure Zvobgo will be wondering where I've gone. He'll want me home for supper. Let me go."

FROM AVENUES TO HIGHLANDS, Tsitsi's Land Cruiser made its way through the potholed road expertly, avoiding the deepest craters. As she moved out of town into the suburbs, she was distracted by the sight of the fields of tall maize that grew on the sides of the road and, when residents found themselves particularly industrious, even in the middle island of the road. She huffed, wishing folk would not display their agrarian industriousness so keenly but rather keep it confined to their own yards.

She drove past the signage and graffiti that implored variously, "ZVAKWANA! SOKWANELE! ENOUGH!", "TIME FOR CHANGE IS NOW!" and "MUDHARA MUST GO!" but ignored the declarations and kept her eyes ahead, concentrating on the cratered road until she had to stop at the robot.

A small, copper-haired street kid appeared at the window of her car. She saw more children like him walking from vehicle to vehicle, hands cupped in the shape of the small bowls used to feed children sadza, others motioning from their mouths to their stomachs. She lowered the window with her right hand as she slipped her left into her handbag to reach for a clump of old Zim dollars. The boy's eager eyes were quick to notice, and he hurriedly alerted two more of his older comrades to the window.

They began clapping cupped hands furiously, thanking her in advance.

"Mazvita, Mama, mazvita."

The oldest one stepped forward to receive the clump of notes, but on noticing their pink colour, he quickly flung them back at her.

She was startled by the harsh, guttural voice that emerged from his small body: "Voetsek! What do you want us to do

59

with this? Wipe our shit? You can't even buy BACOSSI with this!"

The others joined in and rained abuses on her. Alarmed, she quickly rolled up the window. She was sure he was ready to spit at her, he looked so disgusted. Fortunately, it was only a few seconds before the green flash released her and allowed her to make her getaway to her Highlands home.

7

Tsitsi sat alone at the dining table waiting for Zvobgo. She idled away the time eyeing the details of the dining room as she usually did, smiling quietly to herself at the changes she had already made and conjuring up new ways in which she could redecorate the place.

Mary, the house girl, scurried past the doorway, trying to keep herself as invisible as possible.

The house was still but for the cutlery and crockery that tinkered and clinked as it was washed, dried and placed away. The sound of the gossiping voices of the kitchen staff soon drowned out the clinking as they grew restless in the kitchen. They had been ready to serve the 6 p.m. supper for at least twenty minutes now.

Tsitsi had been told that Zvobgo had spent the entire day in his study. She wondered whether she should go and poke her face in and tell him that dinner was ready or have his food dished out and placed in the warmer.

She stood up and then sat down again. No, perhaps not. When she had arrived home from Chiedza's and gone in to greet him, he had pulled his reading spectacles down temporarily and, lifting his eyes from the thick document he was reading, had given no more than a polite, "Hello."

But, as she sat at the table, she reasoned that even at the worst of times he was never late for any appointment and would never upset the routine he had set for himself, so she resolved to go to his study again.

As she neared the study, she heard Zvobgo's voice—indiscernible words to a voiceless confidante. He did not use the telephone often, so this in itself was unusual. He did not raise his voice as he spoke but the intensity of his words, though themselves imperceptible, was palpable.

Kasongo was standing at the open door to the study and, as Tsitsi drew closer he stepped forward to intercept her. But this was unnecessary: on seeing her in the doorway, Zvobgo suddenly stopped talking; drawing the phone's mouthpiece away from his lips, he walked towards her. Before she could open her mouth, he shut the door and continued talking into the mouthpiece.

Tsitsi avoided Kasongo's eyes. Zvobgo had never done this before.

She quickly returned to the dining room and found Robson and Mary packing away the table placements.

"Mr Zvobgo is still coming to eat. Who told you to do this?"

Robson volunteered coolly in Shona, "Mama, we thought that—"

"Don't speak to me in Shona—and don't refer to me as Mama ... I am Mrs Zvobgo to you."

Robson's left eyebrow raised slightly. "Yes, eh, Mr Zvobgo told us he was not eating today, so when you left the table we thought that you were also not eating."

She held his eye, challenging his passive confrontation. "I asked you who told you to pack up because I, as the mother of this house, am the one who will be making decisions here. I do not need you deciding on my behalf."

He sighed as he replaced the fork he had just picked up. He then glanced over at Mary out the corner of his eye and, with impatient hands, ushered her from the room, and followed the girl back out to the kitchen.

Tsitsi was no longer hungry, but still she sat through the entire show again. Robson returned with her food, and because Kasongo was stationed outside Zvobgo's study, Mary fulfilled the role of the second food taster. Tsitsi watched as Robson stepped forward, so beginning the process, which Mary duplicated.

With a lazy forefinger Tsitsi fingered a lump of the steaming sadza. It was still piping hot and she quickly withdrew her finger, pushing it into her mouth to cool the sting. Mary immediately leapt forward to offer cold water to relieve the burn. Smarting from both the sting and embarrassment—an SRB like her should know better, she imagined them both thinking—she got up from the table and hurried off to the bedroom, leaving them to take away the silverware like brides holding unwanted bouquets.

She quickly changed into her nightie and slipped into bed. She tucked in her knees and covered her head with the duvet, turning the incident over and over in her head, wondering what to make of Zvobgo's behaviour.

Why hadn't he told her he would miss supper? Was this not the man who would return at midnight and demand a meal and that she keep him company as he ate? Why hadn't he said anything about not wanting food?

Was someone else cooking for him?

What kind of matters did he have to discuss that required he shut the door on her?

Who was he talking to that he looked so startled when he saw her?

No answers yielded themselves before Tsitsi finally drifted off to sleep with the light still on.

THE SUDDEN BRIGHTNESS when Zvobgo turned on the light woke her. Then, just minutes later, the dark descended again as he switched off the light. She felt his bulge sink into the bed and him pull the duvet up over himself. She didn't open her eyes. She didn't know what mood she would find him in.

He fell asleep quickly. But she remained awake, and only opened her eyes once his snore confirmed that he was in a deep sleep. She turned to face him, observing his profile. His silhouette slowly formed a more distinct shape as her eyes adjusted to the dark. Before long his uneasy staccato breathing carried her back to sleep.

Later in the night, she was brought out of sleep again by the sound of Zvobgo murmuring under his breath and turning in bed. She slunk deeper under the bed covers and slid closer to him to hear his words.

She listened intently as his murmurs became more furious, more anxious, but still she failed to decipher what he was saying.

"Tabitha," she eventually heard.

Her heart tensed. His secretary? She turned so that she could see his face, study it for a clue as to the context. She watched as beads of sweat fell into the creases forming around his brow. Now, as his conversation seemed to intensify further, he was wearing a frown. Remembering the games the hostel girls played on sleeptalkers, she wondered if she could coax clarity out of him by prompting him with questions.

As she edged closer, his eyes shot open. They remained unfocused for only a moment before they turned squarely to Tsitsi. Anger spread across his face, displacing all traces of the vulnerability that were there in his sleep. Anger turned to a look of disgust as if he were looking into the face of a longtime rival.

His stare kept her paralysed, like a fieldmouse cornered by a python. Trapped as she was, she didn't dare say anything. Looking ready to pounce, he didn't break his stare as he got up from the bed.

Then he left the room, leaving her silent and still, unable to sleep for the rest of the night, hurt and confused as she was.

8

T sitsi expected that her petite frame tightly held in her new—and, yes, revealing—evening dress would be met with more enthusiasm when Zvobgo returned home. He had not spent much time at home in the past few weeks, but on this day she took hold of what she saw as an opportunity to reset their relationship with a sultry surprise.

She had taken her time getting dressed, slipping into the dress she had bought in a boutique in Borrowdale earlier that day, smoothing the folds with her palms as she turned in front of the mirror. The dress was a "startling cerise pink" (so the Borrowdale boutique assistant had announced to Tsitsi's delight), chosen for the way it contrasted against her dark skin, something her mother—though she had never concerned herself with worldly preoccupations such as fashion—had always advised because dark colours, she said, would 'dull' her.

When Tsitsi heard his car coming down the gravel driveway, she grabbed his slippers and quickly made her way downstairs, slowing down as she reached the foot of the stairs.

When Zvobgo saw her, he looked confused and then irritated.

"Manheru," he said perfunctorily.

"Manheru, Baba," she greeted him as she knelt to take off his shoes and give him his slippers, making sure his eye caught the dip of her breasts.

"What are you doing?" He pulled her up by the arm. "Jeffreys knows it is his duty to bring my slippers when I get home."

She kept quiet. She had instructed Jeffreys not to meet him at the door when he returned that night.

"And what's the occasion for this dress of yours?" Zvobgo was impatient, tugging at one of the straps.

"I just thought … thought I would make more of an effort to dress for supper like you've suggested," she stumbled, now self-conscious.

"All right then—if this is how you choose to preoccupy your mind all day. But for goodness' sake, wear a cardigan before you catch a cold." He rolled his eyes, before he picked up his briefcase and made his way to his study.

Like a schoolgirl reprimanded by the headmaster, Tsitsi fetched a cardigan from their bedroom. Turning at the mirror as she slipped her arms through the sleeves of the cardigan, she decided to disregard his coldness as a result of stress after the day's work and that she would simply have to work a little harder to remind him of the relief that pleasure could offer, as it had in the past. She picked his favourite perfume and sprayed it onto her neck and breasts, then buttoned her cardigan so that it amplified her cleavage.

At the dinner table they sat in silence. As if to absorb the silence, Kasongo and Robson entered the room. But again the spontaneity she had hoped for was met with banal routine. Robson and Kasongo each tasted the food, before Zvobgo instructed the same procedure for Tsitsi. With a voracious appetite, Zvobgo began to eat.

"Baba," she said nervously, "we have not yet prayed."

He stopped eating and shot her an impatient glance. She hesitated.

"Go on, then, say the prayer if you insist that we can't do anything without the Lord's consent."

His annoyance reminded Tsitsi of the words of Fata Masika, who had claimed that too much education made people arrogant atheists who, because of too much learning and too much science, doubted the existence of the Almighty God, the Alpha, the Omega.

In his frequent warnings against the perils of over-education, Fata Masika had also said that girls who were highly educated did not respect men, even their own husbands. These women had loose morals, he said. They went to bars to dance with other men at night. And when they returned they even wanted to be on top when they made children. And even worse, when they had these children, they could not look after their families because they now felt they were too good for housework! Educating a girl too much was asking for trouble, asking her to become a prostitute.

She recalled one evening, when she had watched Chiedza getting ready to go out, she had told her of Fata Masika's words. At this Chiedza laughed, almost smudging her mascara as tears ran down her blushed cheeks in amusement.

"Tsitsi, my dear, for many families a woman is only really

good enough to do two things. That's to either get married off to a son-in-law for a good number of cows, or, if she so chooses to remain a spinster for the rest of her life, to be free domestic help for the household. So, if that's the case and I have the honour of being disregarded by the likes of Fata Masika, I'm happy to be an educated prostitute."

As Tsitsi remembered this, she wondered if this was something that her mother might have regretted. Over-educating her daughter. Persevering all those years so that now, in the eyes of the Church, the child lived in sin with her traditional husband? Besides the fact that graduates, and their teachers, were now waiters and housegirls in South Africa, Botswana, the UK and whatever other corner of the world offered forex for them to send back home, her living with Zvobgo was probably what caused Mama the most pain.

She bristled at the thoughts, before finally closing her eyes and starting the prayer.

Sign of the Cross.

"Bless us, O Lord, and these Thy gifts, which we are about to receive from Thy bounty, through Christ Our Lord. Amen."

Sign of the Cross.

When she opened her eyes, Zvobgo had already resumed eating. She watched as he ate his food quickly and methodically. "You must not eat like people with no home training, eating like this is a beerhall!" Miss Matsamba, the indomitable matron of her boarding school, would have said before quickly delivering a rap on the knuckles, as part of her endeavours to teach ruffian youth the virtue of values such as cleanliness, punctuality, cooperation, good manners, decorum and all the other aspects of good Christian behaviour. They were forced to sit on their benches, their backs upright so that their spines were straight

69

against the backs of imaginary chairs and were to chew ten times on the right, and ten times on the left before swallowing.

The first bite of sadza burnt Tsitsi's tongue. But she persisted, passing it from one side of her mouth to the other, until the heat was diffused. She flattened the next piece so that the heat would escape.

"When I returned from my jog this morning ..." she mentioned the jog as a reminder that she was working to maintain her figure, a roundabout way of hinting at a body fit to be fucked that night. "... I saw Jeffreys working in the garden and asked him to make the lovely flower arrangements. Did you see the vase in the study?"

She smiled inwardly. Now that she no longer worked, she took pleasure in her ability to manage a household. And not just any household, but this one. Now that she was a little bit more settled in her role as Woman of the Main House, she filled it with many, many shiny trinkets. New glass cabinets with rows and rows of polished dishes and sparkling glassware. Like Mama had once wanted. She decorated and decorated until the entire house was confusedly furnished. Each room had one more cushion, one more chair, table or mirror, than was necessary.

Each time Zvobgo returned, there seemed to be something new to take in. A new portrait. A new rug. A new trinket. A new dinner set. A new mirror. She particularly loved mirrors. There were so many mirrors in the house that he was once prompted to ask, "Are you so vain that you want to see yourself repeated over and over?"

Now all he could manage was, "Yes, Lovely," in between mouthfuls, eyes focused, staring straight through her.

"I thought you might like it."

He continued eating.

"I think it would be a good idea to redo the kitchen. I'm thinking of marble tops. I've also thought we can look at a new ottoman, one that would go better with the lounge and carpet set that I bought last week."

"All right then."

"What do you think?"

"You have your allowance. Is it not enough for this additional ottoman you want?"

"No … I mean, yes, it is enough. I just thought you might be interested in what goes on in the house."

"You're the one who sees this need to redecorate, so do as you please."

She felt a sting in her chest, one that she imagined had been felt by many a woman in her circumstances. She gulped down a big mound of sadza without chewing. As she felt it go down, its heat spread through her throat, her chest, easing the pain of her indignation. Not wanting Zvobgo to see that she was hurt, she drew breath in through her nostrils and closed her eyes briefly, before starting her next attempt at civil conversation.

"And how is your old friend, Gutu?" she asked as nonchalantly as she could.

He sat up at the mention of his old friend, pausing briefly before continuing amid mouthfuls of food.

"There are many wild ideas in people's heads at this time. Gutu is in cohorts with saboteurs and imperialists. But I won't waste time with courts—we will sort him and them out."

As he spoke, Zvobgo ran the back of his fingers against the uncharacteristic stubble on his chin. She took a deep gulp of her water, nodding as if she knew what he was going on about. By now she knew better than to ask.

"He speaks of his contempt for power in that self-righteous tone of his, when we all know what he would give to have his chance to lead."

"Why would he do that? I mean, if he is not genuine?" Tsitsi dared, relieved that she had found a topic he was interested in.

"Because he wants to see us worshipping at his feet." Zvobgo was irritated by her naivete, her inability to see what was so obvious to him.

"Anyway, those men are bloody idiots. Zvidhakwa! Drunk on what little money and power they have. Dancing like monkeys for the peanuts they get from the West. Even an NGO is better. Anyone who follows them is a fool because they are a Mickey Mouse party. The Mbuya from Dodito would not vote for them and nor would they win by popular vote anywhere in the world."

Then the conversation quickly lapsed into silence again. Like clockwork, Robson brought a dish for Zvobgo to wash his hands once he had finished his meal. He rose from the chair.

"Pamusoroi, I must get to bed early, so you will excuse me."

Tsitsi remained in her chair, despondently fingering what remained of her food. What else could she do?

She caught Robson's challenging glare. She immediately instructed him to clear the table, before she got up and followed Zvobgo to their bedroom.

She found the bedside lamps on and Zvobgo awake, reading from a pile of documents on the floor beside the bed. It had been about three months since they had been in each other's conscious presence in their bedroom. Spending nights in his study or at his office, Zvobgo only returned to their room long after she was asleep. She had begun to suspect that this was deliberate.

He didn't look up. She slowed her pace, her movements calculated as she walked to the wardrobe, hoping she might catch his attention and distract him from his reading. She shrugged off the cardigan and pulled out a short nightslip, and then shut the wardrobe door, just loud enough to alert him to her imminent nakedness.

She inserted the corners of the hanger into the sleeves of the cardigan, ensuring that she remained standing in his line of vision should he happen to look up from his documents.

She so wanted to feel the pressure of lustful eyes on her back, so she remained facing the other way, undressing at a deliberately slow pace so that he could catch every movement, every twist of her body.

The nature of their relationship had not been one characterised by shyness, being coy of him seeing her. Eager to build her advantage over Mrs Zvobgo, it was something she was deliberate about. She imagined that Mrs Zvobgo had needed to be coaxed into sex and perhaps changed in the bathroom, away from his watchful eyes. With this thought in mind, she provoked him and he had always welcomed it. She encouraged him to watch openly the dance of seduction she imagined had long been lost in his marriage.

As she began tugging at the zip on the back of her dress, she saw in the mirror on the dressing table that he had looked up, but his eyes were soon back on the papers. She sighed. But she would need his help to get the rest of the zip down.

Maybe that would do it?

As she approached him, she felt her increasing anxiety, precipitated by sweat beads on her forehead, but she worked to compose herself and maintain her otherwise cool façade, her seductive self.

Once at his bedside, she turned around, thrusting her buttocks in his direction so that he could not help but see her soft, round cheeks, the ones he had loved to grab, knead, pound and even slap.

"Commander-in-Chief?" she attempted, looking over her shoulder.

She called him that because, he said, it made him feel like a naughty boy. A call-and-response of sorts as they had become comfortable with each other.

This time her ploy failed to arouse him as it had in the beginning of their affair.

He did not respond to 'Commander-in-Chief.' Instead, he pulled the zip down perfunctorily, annoyed, and quickly returned his attention to his document.

Tsitsi closed her eyes and bit her lip, disappointed that he was not at all receptive to her implicit invitation. She took a moment before slipping off the dress. In the mirror, she watched Zvobgo, who was now sitting up, his eyes fixed on the wall, staring at it with the intensity of a fortune-teller intent on divining some message from an inanimate object. He remained unblinking even as she lingered naked, attempting to obstruct his view, before finally pulling on her nightslip in resignation.

Tsitsi eased into the bed. She stroked his back and he pulled away. She steeled herself, deciding not to read rejection in his lack of response. She continued. She found herself kissing him. Awkwardly. In the art of coaxing, familiar to many old marriages, she suppressed the growing sense of frustration and resentment welling up inside her, reschooling herself in his slowness.

"Please, I am trying to think."

His face was inscrutable. As she pulled her hand back to her body and turned away from him, she wondered what he was thinking.

That was not the first time. When had he lost his appetite for her? When had he started rejecting her advances? What was behind that vacant stare? Was she losing her appeal?

If either of them were to keep up their ends of the bargain, they would have to be clear what those were—and Tsitsi wasn't sure what her half was any more. If it had been to make sure he was physically satisfied, there was clearly something preventing her from doing so. And if she wasn't fulfilling hers, would that mean he was no longer obligated to keep up what had been tacitly agreed as his?

She shut her eyes, hot tears making their way down her cheeks. She covered her mouth to suppress the sound of her heavy breathing. Finally, when the tears subsided, Tsitsi reached to the side table and felt for her sleeping tablets and a glass of water. She gulped, swallowed and waited for sleep to rescue her from the menacing questions that plagued her.

THE RING of the landline woke Tsitsi with a start. Nowadays, phone calls for Zvobgo at odd hours were another thing to which she had grown accustomed. When he was there, his cellphone and the landline rang constantly. Whenever she picked up the landline, there was a different voice, male or female, asking for him. He always took the calls in his study. And each time she answered to a female voice, she was tempted to listen in from the bedroom. She was wary of simply dismissing them all as work-related calls, as Mrs Zvobgo had seemed to do when she, Tsitsi, was the one calling.

She looked at her watch: 5:30. Zvobgo was not in bed. The ring lasted just briefly before it stopped. Zvobgo must have picked it up in his study. Tsitsi gently lifted the receiver from its cradle and heard Zvobgo's voice on the other end. She recognised the other flat, unattractive voice as that of Tabitha. What was she doing talking to Zvobgo at this hour?

They spoke with ease and familiarity. His voice had none of the strain that he now so often displayed; in fact, he sounded relieved to hear her voice.

Although she couldn't make out much of the content of their conversation, the way they spoke struck her with suspicion.

She caught the end of their conversation.

"Thank you, Tabitha. I will do that."

Tsitsi put the phone down hard on its receiver. She fumbled around in her handbag for her cellphone, and messaged Chiedza: Hie Chi, whts up? Mt @ Tropicana 2night?

9

———

"So," Chiedza announced dramatically as she sat down on a chair at their usual table, "I'm here with my sugar daddy, Jonathan, the American spy I met at Borrowdale Race Course."

"A spy? ChiChi, what kind of movie are you living in?" Tsitsi scrunched her nose.

"Yes, Tsitsi, a spy! You think Zvobgo and his crew are just paranoid? This Jonathan, he's a real-deal spy."

"So if he's the real deal, what's he doing with you?"

"I think he has jungle fever," she threw back her head and began to cackle. "I even asked him what his fascination with black women is. Told him that I'm sure that black, white and even purple women for that matter, have the same anatomy. He just laughed and grabbed my bum. Anyway, he's in a meeting in one of the rooms here, so he told me to keep myself entertained until he's done. And then, you know ..."

Chiedza's voice grated with exasperation. She used her eyes to great effect. She loved to dramatise everything she said. She pretended to gag as she rummaged through her handbag for a packet of cigarettes. Tsitsi watched as Chiedza lit up, the smoke curling high up to the chandelier above them. She thought about how all of this, made even more deplorable with the impending addition of alcohol, would have scandalised her mother and, not too long ago, her too.

Aside from the release, Chiedza smoked as a way to keep the weight off. "You know I don't have curves like you, Tsitsi. Ndikafuta, I will never become a Coke bottle," she said as she mimed the shape of the bottle with her hands. "Instead, I'll be more like a fridge or a bottle of Mazoe!" She would, she said, make a large fridge too—like the one Tsitsi had bought for Mama and Sekuru Dickson—and burst into laughter.

Chiedza's make-up was painted on in bold, garish colours as if to implicate her American lover in a scuffle the previous night. Tsitsi herself was unrecognisable from her usual, traditional guise. She had her twelve-inch weave brushed out in full display and wore a tight-fitting dress. In any case, it didn't really matter if she was recognised as Zvobgo's Live-In-Girlfriend, because the diplomats, forex dealers, authorised journalists and the like, all tacitly agreed to a code of self-censorship or risked implicating themselves in the immorality.

Chiedza had always been industrious. When her older sister, Netsai, had been an air hostess with Air Zimbabwe, she had been one of the first to begin importing goods from London.

She applied the same kind of diligence to her beauty. She was the kind of woman who had an immediate effect on men, simply because her entire being, her whole demeanour, was sexual. And so she often dispensed with rules of courtship, relying on an innate ability to approach men directly and still have them pursue her after the first encounter. When she had worked as a waitress, it was for what she called 'the networking opportunity.' According to Chiedza, it was better than being a secretary. Her hours were flexible, for one. And, of course, she could pick and choose. She could afford to be non-committal—there was a greater variety of men available to her, so she could be discriminating in her choices.

On quiet days, when the restaurant manager was not there, she often used to take the patrons' orders before sitting down at the table with them, a move that always disarmed them and, for many, elicited a nervous sense of excitement at her show of assertiveness, a hint of sexual confidence and prowess. The kind of show that let them know that this was a woman who could ride on top. For those with imagination, her build lent itself to the image of a sturdy mare, one they would not need to be gentle with, one they could ride and be rough with, feeling her take, and enjoy, all of them, unlike the gentle and fragile virgins they had married.

Chiedza called a waiter to their table. "Whisky on the rocks, please."

"Just a Coke for me."

"Nhai iwe, Tsitsi, I thought you asked me to come out for drinks?" Chiedza pulled the waiter's arm. "You remind me," she said to Tsitsi, "of the religious zealot you used to be." She turned to the waiter. "She'll have the same. Just add lime for taste."

Tsitsi tried to object, but she knew that this was all beyond her control and it wasn't long before their waiter was returning with their fourth round. By then she no longer noticed. And when the waiter came back with their fifth,

Tsitsi took her drink right off his tray before he had the chance to set it down.

On an inebriated wave, Tsitsi continued her soliloquy. She felt self-conscious of the repetition, but the relief from unburdening herself got the better of her.

"Shuwa, Chiedza," she paused to consider her words, "I have it better than those holier-than-thou women with their marriages."

"You know, T, I took a psychology course for two semesters." Chiedza leaned forward, placing her arms on the table, so that Tsitsi could smell her whisky-and-smoke-laced breath, "And do you know what was the most important lesson that I learnt?"

Tsitsi shook her now heavy head.

"I'll tell you, the most important thing that I learnt was not from a textbook, but from experience. It's that the beautiful thing about the mind is that if you tell yourself a lie enough times, you will start believing it. The Catholic saint who dreamed of a big white wedding has talked herself into living in sin."

"Chiedza—"

"Look, whatever keeps you happy, my dear. And, most importantly, whatever keeps you fed in this upside-down BACOSSI economy, handiti?"

Tsitsi held her head in her hands and then looked up, forcing a smile. "Chi, it's easier this way. He's my husband now."

Chiedza stubbed her cigarette in the ashtray, then fished for another in her bag. Despite a number of strikes, the match wouldn't light. She got up and approached the next table with the confidence of a woman who is used to having her way with men— men who are in fact looking to be tempted.

The men at the next table—old white men with skin pink from a day in the Sunshine City—smoking cigars, happily obliged, even offering her a cigar, not only because Chiedza was possibly the central character to a fantasy they wished to act out, Tsitsi guessed, but also because of the easy camaraderie of smokers that never ceased to amaze Tsitsi.

One of the men happily produced a lighter, and popped it, igniting the flame. Chiedza bent over, putting the cigarette already in her mouth to it, and inhaled. Immediately, she seemed to come back into focus, taking deep pleasure in the fumes.

"Thanks ka?" she winked at them.

"Anytime, babe."

"Why don't you join us?" his friend asked.

"Next time," she glanced back over her shoulder, smug with satisfaction. Settled back in her seat, Chiedza remained quiet for a short time, inhaling the smoke from her cigarette before continuing.

"The most difficult kind of honesty is honesty with yourself, Tsitsi—you know that." Chiedza drank deeply before leaning in towards her. "But tell me, you must be getting bored, lying under the same septuagenarian?"

"No. Not really." Tsitsi averted her eyes.

"Zvenyu! He's that good, huh? Rather! I have to say, I didn't see it coming from that potbelly."

"No. We haven't—" her speech slowed as she struggled to find the words jumping around in her head, which was now pounding with a bad headache.

"You haven't what?"

She straightened herself and raised her hand for their waiter. "Bring me some water, please."

"Tsitsi, what? You haven't what?"

"Whatever I say can and will be used against me. I hereby invoke my Miranda Rights to remain silent under questioning."

Chiedza laughed heartily, almost choking on her whisky.

"What? Your Miranda Rights! Don't make me laugh!"

Tsitsi smiled, "I took a law course too, you know."

"I am your friend and have a right to know. Where there is a conflict, The Right of the Friend to Know takes precedence over the Miranda Rights."

Tsitsi remained silent until the waiter returned with the glass. She gulped down the water and immediately called for another. Now more in control of the words in her head, she began again.

"Chiedza, Zvobgo and I haven't done it in a while."

She said the words quickly in the hope that they would float up, disappear lightly into the air with her friend's cigarette smoke, but Chiedza latched onto them.

"Wow, so His Excellency His Grace Comrade Zvobgo is a keeper. You stinge him and he doesn't kick you out?"

"No, Chi, he's been focused on other things."

"Other things?" Chiedza narrowed her eyes. "You mean other women? Shamaz, I've been with enough men to know that a man has to eat." She sat her glass down and called for the waiter again. "Imwe whisky, Sekuru."

Tsitsi broke eye contact. "No. He wouldn't."

"Ha, Tsitsi, are you saying our man is like Banana?"

The thought flitted through her brain, but she quickly suppressed it. "No, no, Chi—I know he likes women."

Chiedza did not seem convinced. "My dear, what makes you think you are so exceptional?"

"Never mind, Chiedza. It's nothing. Really, nothing." Even her own insistence struck her as suspicious. She forced an approximation of a laugh, "I know my Zvobgo wouldn't do anything, okay?"

"And why not? If he could do it to her, he can do it to you."

Chiedza carried on oblivious as Tsitsi remained silent, the dull throb in her head beginning to surface again. She felt dizzy.

A burly man in a safari suit at the adjacent table spoke in nasal tones, "Look, Montreaux, the $300 000 US-made solar-powered irrigation system is rusting in a shed because they can't maintain the damn thing and because they have that 'Look East' policy. So you can judge for yourself."

Said the man next to him, "I'm a bit more optimistic. Though they're playing an underhand game, I think this election will be a breakthrough. I can't go into the specifics but there are encouraging signs. The cracks are beginning to show."

The two were addressing a taller colleague who was jotting down parts of their conversation on a dog-eared notepad. A mop of black hair, wet and greying at the edges, nose sunburnt and flaking, chest hairs peeking out of his white shirt. The archetypal Brit, born and bred, who had discovered this bit of Empire relatively late in life but nonetheless embodied a familiar colonial entitlement to the now independent territory, for it held a sense of romance and adventure ripe for mid-life crises. Romance held in the stubborn remnants of Rhodesia memorialised in a good number of British street names (Rotten Row included) that had managed to dodge the indignity of new native names while the natives themselves remained "extremely friendly and cheerful, which is remarkable under the circumstances," "always joking," "very hardworking, more so than the blacks from South Africa and Zambia I've encountered" and, like the noble savages so deigned by the British, "so well educated." Adventure held in the TIA-ness of 'The Decay of Africa' and in the danger of imminent deportation for reporting the kind of things they were discussing now as the territory continued on its about-turn from the settlement secured by old Lord Soames.

Tsitsi decided she would report this to Zvobgo, and then turned back to Chiedza.

Chiedza took a long drag of her cigarette.

"Or …" Chiedza raised her finger, and her eyes grew bigger. "I've studied this before, I've got it!" She clapped her hands, startling the tables around them. "It's necrophilia! He must be necrophillic. Where do you think all those missing people go to if they can't be found at Mbudzi cemetery?" she said excitedly before dropping her voice to a whisper. "Fulfilling a fetish? Perhaps your living flesh can never satisfy him."

Hot tears pushed their way to Tsitsi's eye sockets as she felt a surge of anger. Before she could string the words to tell Chiedza off for her insensitivity, her head began to pound even harder, paralysing her into resignation. She closed her eyes until the surge slowed, and found enough strength to stand up from her seat.

"Chiedza, you don't need to act so happy at my situation." Tsitsi's eyes shone. She surprised herself with her words. She had never voiced that there was a 'situation.' She couldn't say it to Chiedza. By giving it a name, she felt she would give it the power to manifest itself and flourish in reality. If, instead, it remained in the limbo of unspoken words, it could surely be contained and eventually disappear of its own.

She felt the sensation she often felt when she drank, as if someone was pouring cement into her head. With these thoughts, it felt heavier and heavier.

"I'm not some little girl, a child, or someone's whore. I'm a woman. A respectable one, Chiedza, so these things can't concern me."

Chiedza glanced at the adjacent table, checking to see if anyone had heard, and then laughed.

"You know, Tsitsi, you are so quick to point out that you are not a prostitute. I just want to laugh because you are just falling into rank. You all should spare us your 'morality' that lauds 'women' over the supposedly lesser 'whores' and 'girls.' That's how society sees us. That's how you see us. You want it to be that we are like coal, only to be loved in the dark and tossed like ashes come morning."

She looked again at the table alongside, her hands fidgeting in her lap, manicured nails scraping at the buckle of her purse. Tsitsi could see tears well up in her friend's eyes.

"You look at me, and you judge me. And I just want to ask, for what? I am fully in control. No one has a gun to my head. Why can't this be my profession, one I have chosen for myself? I tell you, prostitutes are professional in their skills and practise it like the vocation of true apostles—and why shouldn't they? What's so different from the accountant or the doctor selling his time? I ended up in this profession in the same way someone might end up being a lawyer because they couldn't get into engineering or dentistry, or because they couldn't get into medicine, or even a banker who grew up telling everyone they want to be a soccer player. They do those things because that was what was available for their talents and their circumstances at the time. But do we pity them? No, because that's lif—"

"Chiedza, I didn't me—"

"No, Tsitsi, chimboteerera. You of all people know the dreams that I had. The dreams that you had. Remember? I was going to be a businesswoman. I was going to be the chairwoman of Dairiboard, of African Sun, of all those ZSE companies. You wanted to be at the Reserve Bank, working on monetary policy and foreign exchange controls. But when we left UZ, things changed—the only spaces open were the NGO and the ministry. And even that didn't work. We had responsibilities to take care of, and this is where we are. Ndohupenyu hwacho, Tsitsi."

Words Mama had repeated so often throughout Tsitsi's childhood. Ndohupenyu hwacho.

Chiedza's eyes shone. She had long since lost her cheerfulness. Tsitsi wasn't sure if it was the alcohol that had made her so sensitive, so emotional, but she was embarrassed and felt selfish for trying to unburden her own anxieties. She sat down again, pretending not to notice that Chiedza was upset, trying to make light of their current situation.

"Remember what we used to say in residence?" Chiedza didn't answer, but Tsitsi persevered. "When things got tough, we would always say: 'That is that. Sadza repabhodhingi.'"

She laughed nervously, hoping that her invocation of their varsity days would cheer Chiedza up. Eventually, she broke into a small laugh.

"Eii sha, but we suffered, didn't we? Sadza nebeans. Sadza necabbage. Sadza nemapotatoes."

Chiedza eventually gave in and added, "Vakomana, sadza, sadza, sadza. When we were lucky, sadza nemazai."

They giggled together as if they were in their Swinton room. Feeling a little more sober and that the situation had been diffused, even just marginally, Tsitsi stood up again.

"ChiChi, it's late. Zvobgo will be waiting for me. I'm sure James Bond is waiting for you too."

Chiedza rose to peck Tsitsi goodbye, "Well, you know, I like pushing my men to their limits. The longer he waits the better."

She saw the leaks of tears under Tsitsi eyes and wiped them away tenderly with her thumbs, kissing her on her cheek, reminding Tsitsi of the many times Chiedza had consoled her in their dorm room.

"See, Tsitsi? It's easier when he's an attached superior and stays that way. It's when he starts suffocating me and makes too many demands that I leave. Simple. There isn't a shortage of horny old men. For that matter, even young ones."

Before Tsitsi could respond, their waiter jogged clumsily over to their table. Fearing they were attempting to dodge the bill, he couldn't afford the dignity of a graceful walk.

"Don't worry, Sekuru, tichiri tese. I'm not going anywhere for a while. I'm sure you'll have fun keeping me company," said Chiedza with a wink.

He didn't respond with the polite laughter of a grateful servant. He was not the cheerful and obedient servant their money had promised them. Instead he obliged with no more than a tight smile, which soon returned to a sour look of resentment, characteristic of a quick, intelligent mind trapped in the routine of menial tasks. He did what he was asked to do with a cold efficiency, nothing more.

"I'll see you, Chiedza," Tsitsi said.

As she drove home, she tried to shrug off Chiedza's words, but they managed to linger and set themselves deep in her conscience. If Zvobgo could do it to Mrs Zvobgo, surely he could do it to her? It would be history repeating itself.

But this was different, she thought. His wife could well afford to respond to the rejection and the humiliation of infidelity by fleeing to Malaysia to live with their thirty-something-year-old daughters. If Zvobgo left Tsitsi, she would be destitute.

She toyed with the idea of his other colleagues, but she quickly dismissed the notion. They were all too busy with their current Small Houses and, even if they did take her in, she was sure they would not look after Sekuru and Mama in the way that Zvobgo did.

She had everything but that elusive certificate. Only important, because with titles come obligations, and more importantly, with rights. Rights and claims to property. Without that, what would she do about Mama and Sekuru? At best, she would be referred to Zvobgo's relatives or to the traditional courts.

She snuck into the darkened bedroom without switching on the lights for fear of waking Zvobgo. The last thing she wanted to do was trigger a torrent of questions. She slipped off her dress and, without bothering to get her nightslip, sunk slowly into bed. Not hearing even a grunt from Zvobgo's side of the bed, she reached out but felt only cold sheets. She remembered now that he had told her he was to be spending a few nights away with the rest of the executive members. She had forgotten. She felt disappointed, foolish, for having said all she had to Chiedza.

CHIEDZA'S WORDS fell over Tsitsi and hung there the entire time Zvobgo was away.

Maybe she could confront him? She liked the idea, thinking of how he would then throw a show of telling her that it was untrue and would go to great lengths to reassure her of his commitment to her.

Chiedza kept saying that Tsitsi should be honest with herself, but if she were honest, the more she thought about his behaviour, the less sure she was that he would go to any lengths at all to reassure her. In fact, if she really thought about it, she couldn't say she would have been opposed to being taken in as a second wife. She could easily have accepted being a co-wife and having to defer to Mrs Zvobgo as the senior wife. She could have learnt a lot from her. And Tabitha, the most junior wife, would in turn have to defer to her. He would just have to seek permission from her and Mrs Zvobgo. He would have to consult the two of them if he wanted to take a new wife, and they would have the power to veto it if they found she would upset the balance of their home. For her part, though, she wouldn't mind how many he brought in, as long as she was looked after. Theirs would not have been the first polygamous home. Yes, the three of them could quite easily have become co-wives.

Maybe that would have been better. If she had opened him up to that possibility, then she wouldn't now be in a situation where another woman threatened her place in the household. Mama would have had to understand. Maybe she could suggest the idea to him?

An alternative would be that he would calmly explain to her that their relationship had deteriorated. That he, within less than two years, had already lost his natural inclination for the pleasures of her flesh. He was still fond of her, so they would now be partners. He would reassure her that just because they no longer shared a bed did not mean she would have to be kicked out of the house. It just meant that they had acknowledged that they were not romantic partners and they could live in separate rooms. And of course he was happy to keep her in his care. They would now live in perfect sexless harmony. A harmony that need not be disturbed as it would be easier than to have to renegotiate their lives completely.

Or maybe he would keep her and continue to have these other women. She would assume the role of a Long-Suffering Wife who would look dispassionately as he brought whore after whore into their house. As a Long-Suffering Wife, she would take it all in with dignity.

She felt a sharp sense of lucidity in her jealousy. She struggled to keep it contained in a corner of her heart, and soon was consumed by it.

The first thing she did the next morning was to call Tabitha at the office. As she dialled, she felt a sense of panic build up in her ... What was it that she really intended to say? Confront the woman? Warn her to leave her man alone? Tell her about being co-wives?

"She isn't in," said the receptionist. "She's at the executive conference."

This only seemed further confirmation of Tsitsi's already rampant suspicions. She felt her heart burn with certainty, no longer simply an inkling. Now she had no choice but to accept Chiedza's judgement. She now felt an odd sense of kinship with Mrs Zvobgo and, with that, came a belated sense of remorse for her own actions.

Of course she could not tell Chiedza. She would suffer in silence. That would be part of her penance.

10

There wasa massof expectant parishioners—children and adults—standing outside the open front doors of a church. The bright sun in a cloudless blue sky reigning over the auspicious day, a day for celebration.

Tsitsi saw a bride and, accompanying her, their arms linked, a man she guessed was her father in a modest grey suit topped off with a white carnation to match the bouquet held by the bride. She looked again and saw that the man could not have been the bride's father because they were not entering the church—they were leaving it. They stood smiling at the top of the steps. The man must be the groom, she thought. They now made their way down, ducking as the crowd threw rice, grains lodging themselves in the bride's coiffed hair.

Soon the crowd was under a white marquee, waiting in single file for their turn to have officious aunties dish up plates of rice, sadza, roast chicken, beef stew, coleslaw and potato salad. Excitable children ran around giddy from the sugar in the fizzy drinks, some spilling on unimpressed guests. The newlyweds presided over the festivities at a table at the back of the marquee.

———————

TSITSI WAS WOKEN up by the sound of Zvobgo's alarm clock, which she hadn't deactivated despite his being away.

It was still dark, so she stayed in bed and attempted to go back to sleep. But, she was restless and could not still her thoughts. The dream did not offer Tsitsi much in the way of the relief, or even the hope that it would—or could—come true; instead, it brought a new sense of burning urgency to her plight.

Lying under the duvet, in Zvobgo's king-sized bed, in his, her, Highlands home, Tsitsi thought about the day when she last had this burning feeling. The day a couple of years ago when she had disregarded Mama's fatalism and decided that she would take matters into her own hands.

———————

IT HAD BEEN early evening on a Friday, month-end Friday, which meant she had just received her meagre salary. She sat on the bed she shared with Mama, tired, despondent after the mind-boggling busyness of work and the kombi commute from town where she had given the rude hwindi the equivalent of half her salary.

If she had been conditioned differently, things would have been better, she had thought. If she had felt like the others, she could have found comfort in the knowledge that they were not choking on expectations of great things.

Because, as Mama, and now Chiedza, would say, "Ndohupenyu hwacho."

That was life. It was just like that. Nothing to be done about it.

She chewed on the words until she had extracted all possible meaning.

No matter how she tried to digest them, although she was certainly not alone in her plight, she could not help but personalise them. Perhaps this was the same sort of exceptionalism that had seen her succeed all throughout her school years.

Sekuru had returned to his position on the boulder outside Mama's room after having accompanied Mama to church for an All Night Vigil for the Country. He was playing his favourite tape loudly which he would rewind and repeat for the rest of the night, playing it to his heart's content because his sister was not around to complain.

She looked on pitifully at Sekuru Dickson, wearing his old uniform.

Even though he was already of retirement age when he lost his job, he still could not bear to return kumusha. He had long ago stopped visiting his wife and three adult children, as part of a self-imposed economic exile of sorts. Instead his wife and children visited him at his sister's home kuTown.

Perhaps because after all those years working hard in town, he had expected a different turn of luck. A turn of luck that would have seen him a supervisor, a manager, a Something Important. He had worked hard, diligently, showing initiative where he could:

"Manager, on pension day the queues for the pensioners are so long and many of them get tired, why don't we try and have a special desk for the pensioners?"

"It doesn't hurt to try! Great idea, Dickson, thank you!"

"Manager, when I help the customers, especially the ones from the village, fill in the forms I always have to explain what the big English words mean, why don't we try and print forms in Shona?"

"It doesn't hurt to try! Great idea, Dickson, thank you!"

"Manager, I have seen when the school children come out of class, they have lots of pocket money and they spend it all on ice cream, freezits and maputi. I can only imagine what I would have done with so much pocket money! Why don't we try and go to schools to talk to the children about opening savings accounts?"

"It doesn't hurt to try! Great idea, Dickson, thank you!"

They tried all of the suggestions! They loved them all! And yet they did not advance.

Perhaps the longer the self-imposed exile, the more important he wanted—and needed—his Return to be.

Anyone who had not known better would have thought that the reason he did not return was that he was like one of those Benz businessmen or Meikles ministers who had grown up in 'the tribal trust lands,' and yet as soon as they had gained a foothold in Harare, Mutare or Bulawayo, would not return. For them, progress meant never having to return. To go back was to regress.

No, it was just that Sekuru Dickson had had a different picture of how he would have returned.

Imagine, all those years in town! He would return kumusha, the Triumphant Town Returnee. The Triumphant Town Returnee from Harare, Mutare, Bulawayo, Johannesburg, Cape Town, Gaborone, Lusaka and maybe even London, ready kugadzira misha.

Ready kugadzira misha, as soon as he stepped off the bus PaNingirinkini.

As soon as he stepped off the bus PaNingirinkini, he would be The Triumphant Returnee from Harare, Mutare, Bulawayo, Johannesburg, Cape Town, Gaborone, Lusaka and maybe even London.

He would be The Triumphant Returnee from Harare, Mutare, Bulawayo, Johannesburg, Cape Town, Gaborone, Lusaka and maybe even London with a suitcase full of progress.

With a suitcase full of progress, packed with a new jarata roof for the dundroom, a new polished cement floor in the kitchen for Amai, a new two-in-one blanket, a new bicycle, new books for the grandchildren, new ZhingZhong clothes for everyone and a new radio for himself.

Packed with a new jarata roof for the dundroom, a new polished cement floor in the kitchen for Mai Mutumwa, a new mughodhi closer to her kitchen, a new lick of paint, a new two-in-one blanket, a new bicycle, new books for the grandchildren, new ZhingZhong clothes for everyone and a new radio for himself, he would be greeted with open arms.

He would be greeted with open arms, "Tigashire! Tigashire! Mauya! Mauya! The Triumphant Returnee from Harare, Mutare, Bulawayo, Johannesburg, Cape Town, Gaborone, Lusaka and maybe even London with a suitcase full of progress: a new jarata roof for the dundroom, a new polished cement floor in the kitchen for his wife Mai Mutumwa, a new mughodi closer to her kitchen, a new two-in-one blanket, a new bicycle, new books for the grandchildren, new ZhingZhong clothes for everyone and a new radio for himself! Mauya nebudiriro!"

Budiriro he would not bring.

Instead, he would return, empty handed, a burden to his wife and the three adult children who variously worked and loitered around the bottle stores, butchers and hardware stores PaNingirinkini. Not a Triumphant Returnee, but perhaps a Burdensome Baranzi.

For that, he could not bear to return.

He was sure the neighbours muline looked at his wife, Mai Mutumwa, in pity. He was sure the pity and the disdain travelled down through each wife muline who would relish the opportunity to have their say on the matter.

Mai George would start:

"Nhai, what kind of a husband does Mai Mutumwa have? It has been years since he returned to help her plough, to help her sow, to help her? It's as if he is working kuJubheki or Botswana or Zambia. He is just here, padyo apa paHarare! Surely he can afford to climb a bus to come help his wife?"

Next Mai Miriam:

"Mai Mutumwa, what happened to that man? He used to send big amounts of money? She was so proud! Zvakatanga achidada, zvikapedzesera akuvhaira!"

Then Mai Tsungi:

"Shuva, where is that man of hers? That one who used to buy new clothes for Mutumwa, Magona and Masimba every time they passed! Shuwa! When each of them passed A-levels, we didn't hear the end of it! Even when muzukuru wake Tsitsi passed we were the first to know! Nhai, where is that man now?"

And finally Mai MaTwins:

"Are you sure he isn't eating that money with a mainini ikoko kuTown? Or worse, nemahure? I'm convinced! Why else hasn't he returned?"

Sekuru Dickson imagined, the men muline, especially the ones who were his age-mates, were not to be outdone.

Baba Tsungi would start:

"Mufunge, when we were young boys Dickson was so proud! Now he is nowhere to be seen."

Next Baba Miriam:

"That's true! Dickson aidya mabee! He used to beat us all at school! He was always reading! Even when we would herd cattle—his books would come with us! When we had long gone to find work, he persevered until Form 2! We didn't see the end of that certificate! Zvakatanga achidada, zvikapedzesera akuvhaira!"

Then Baba Blessing:

"With that certificate, he went to Harare long before any of us and yet he is still there. Doing what, we don't know."

Baba Chaguma:

"Is he not staying with his sister?"

And finally, Baba MaTwins:

"That's what they say. Asi, mawonero angu ndeekuti, he has found a nice, young, mainini in town and now he is no longer interested in his old wife. What else could it be? If not that, he is eating his money nemahure. I'm convinced! Why else hasn't he returned?"

TSITSI SAT LISTENING to Karikoga and his old backing vocalist sing plaintively together from the window, asking if they too would receive their chance, their toehold in life, just like vaye vaye vakaita mhanza yekukwirepo pamusoro.

At the ministry she had tried concerning herself with the job alone, filling her mind with the demands of a rudimentary desk job. But, really, she could do it all in less than two hours. Even when she found ways to try to drag out her duties, fill her day, still that would only extend it by another two hours. Two more hours filled with mindless busyness.

Busy, busy. Ordering, reordering and refilling. Refilling water jugs. Emptying water into plants. Emptying water into plants. Sorting and alphabetising. Sorting and alphabetising. Opening mail, closing mail, marking unread. Opening mail, closing mail, marking unread. Checking the time. Opening mail, closing mail, marking unread. Sorting and alphabetising. Sorting and alphabetising. Refilling water jugs. Ordering, reordering and refiling. Busy, busy.

She even began to believe it all herself. She had to, so that when Sekuru and Mama asked their Dear Daughter what she had done at work that day, she could say, with an air of self-importance, that they wouldn't understand even if she explained. But all they needed to know was that their daughter was busy. This busyness had to be proven by the dishevelled look she had begun to cultivate. She would take pleasure when Mama, concerned, asked after her and she could respond with a righteous shrug, "What can I do, Mama? That's the job. I can't even think about eating, let alone my hair, when I am there. I am just so busy."

Maybe, like the others in the office, she could have come in at 8 a.m., placed her jacket on her chair, left the office to do her dealings in town and returned at 5 p.m. to pick up the jacket. That was the newly formed punch-in system, an appropriate proxy for productivity.

But she had seen things differently then. She would be damned if someone came to look for Zvobgo and she was not there. This job, as mindless as it was, she could not afford to lose. Too many would scramble to snatch it away from her if she lost her grip on it. She couldn't. She had to be grateful. A job was a job. The time for careers and passions was gone. Hunger pangs displaced ambition.

In her despair she had consoled herself that at least it was not back-breaking physical work.

By the end of the month, she was sure she would go out of her mind. She had looked at her payslip and then at Sekuru mournfully singing "Mugove," asking once more if the Dear Lord would indeed let him have his fair share while alive? Those who prospered pushed him around, and yet he had nothing! Tsitsi began to laugh hysterically as Sekuru and Karikoga pressed on.

Tinongotsikirirwa! A month's pay that lasted two days. Two days. Two days! Tichingotsikirirwa! She felt her stomach muscles cramping at the insanity. Tinongoshandiswa nhando! How painfully appropriate the words of these two men were at this moment. Tichingofondotswa!

Oh God, two days, she sighed. Just two days and it was gone! Wha! As if she had been carefree, living it up on the town, pushing back a now-sweaty freshly sewn twelve-inch with newly set long nails as she gyrated to Winky D, B.O.P., Mafikizolo or an old Kanda Bongo Man, depending on the mood of the DJ or sometimes even the taste of a man just trying to impress his well-heeled daij, all the while refusing to have any man buy her drinks because she was independent and, as she playfully mouthed, she had self-R-E-S-P-E-C-T, waving an authoritative index finger, before turning to hit the bar to buy rounds for the entire hall, who would then salute to the Good Life, from which she would come crashing down hard and broke, humbled into eating nyimo and maputi for the rest of the month with the same now-tired-looking weave and broken acrylics.

That would have been better, yes, because at least she would have had some joy from her money. She could have had one month's work devoted to one night's entertainment. But here there was none of that. Two days, two days, two days and only a sense of mocking despair and austerity to show for it. Nothing, nothing, nothing. Zero. Naught. Like the mocking score showing all, especially Tsitsi, the company bursar, Mama and Sekuru, that she had failed in the test of life.

It was like she had been playing nhodo with her life, foolishly trying to outsmart an imaginary playmate named Fate.

"Wabira!" she would have shouted to Fate. She was sure these were not the rules they had agreed to. Shuwa, shuwa, she was sure. She was supposed to win. Like Karikoga, she just wanted her fair share from the world, yet she was losing as she clumsily tried to toss and catch her little stones and failed.

Fate, smiling and menacing, would continue playing, skilfully tossing and catching her set of little stones, and say smugly, "Charovedzera charovedzera, gudo rakakwira mawere kwasviba."

Practice makes perfect? What a thing to say when the game was clearly not in her favour! Her stones, she was sure, were heavier than those dealt to Fate. This unfairness would cause Tsitsi to denounce her friendship with this playmate Fate, who she had come to know as not understanding and self-sacrificing, saying: "Futi, hausi shamwari yangu!"

She chuckled even more hysterically at the last thought, quickly grabbing a pillow to cover her mouth, lest Sekuru hear her and call for eHlangeni. She had been leaning on her elbow as she laughed almost soundlessly for fear that any sound might indicate that she was in pain. Sekuru and Karikoga lamented the pain that they too shared with Tsitsi. Moyo yavo yairwadza kuti nguva dzose ndivo wekunyengerera sei Mambo? Why was it always them? Tsitsi began to laugh. How could she have thought she was alone in her despair?

How foolish of her! How arrogant!

She laughed so much that her stomach muscles began to ache and, unable to steady herself quickly enough, she keeled over so that her head struck the wall. The impact was hard and soon had the laughing maniac crying like a child. She wasn't one to cry readily at physical injury, but this came as a pretext, to free the tears of desperation that had been building up within her. The flood burst her inner walls of strength and shook her body. She cried pathetically and thoughtlessly for nearly an hour, until she had a pounding headache. Her temples throbbed as she held herself in an awkward embrace.

Silently, she wondered whether this was the same desperation, the same sense of impotence that grips many men by their shirts, their T-shirts, their work vests, gripping them equally hard, shaking them and leading them to drink, to beating or the noose. Was this it?

Karikoga and Sekuru seemingly answered her question, she was sure with shrugging shoulders—there was no one who knew the answer, nor the day it would come.

This was the kind of impotence, futility, that blanketed the world in cynicism. The feeling of impotence that crept up on her whenever she saw children making their way to school, faithfully dressed in their white socks and black shoes, disproportionately sized satchels on their backs, heavy with books, compelling her to ask what they were being offered as the reason for having to wake up at some ungodly hour in order to struggle through lessons while ignoring grumbling stomachs. The same sense of impotence that made her want to cry at the cruel joke teachers, parents and the world played on these innocent souls when they told them that they could be whatever they wanted to be. It was as if they had forgotten that great disappointment that had slowly crept up on them, as dreams of self-actualisation morphed into thoughts of stomach actualisation, sacrificed in order to put food on the table.

She wanted to grab the shoulders of those parents and ask them, what was the purpose of preparing these children for a life that was not intended for them? Perhaps it is all no more than a cruel joke played in the spirit of that false joviality, sarcasm and self-deprecation that people adopt so readily, chuckling and giggling heartily, squealing like children, their eyes shut tight in sweet ecstasy so that they do not see or feel the despair of their miserable, chaotic realities. A tranquiliser against the painful anxiety of scarcity when they had expectant mouths to feed.

She continued to cry for a time, achieving nothing more than unburdening her spirit of the yoke of the world's demands. She felt powerless to do anything else.

All the while her mother's voice chanted like a litany, mismatched against Karikoga's beat, "Women can't cry when they must get on." As the tears in her eyes dried, Tsitsi's eyes became quick and sharp with opportunism. She wiped what remained of her tears with the back of her hand and sat up.

Together the two singers painfully prodded her as they invoked her dear mother. When would her mother thank her? Thank her totem? Indeed she asked herself, ndovapei kuti vagonditendawo? She too wanted to hear her praise name, maita Mukumbudzi! Maita veshungu!

If she wanted to hear it, she had to get on.

Yes, she had to get on. Her mother, too, wanted to bask in the satisfaction of having successfully raised and educated a child. Her mother would also want to have something to show for it. She thought about Karikoga's words again: Amai vangu vanoda kutendawo. Havachaziva nekudetemba mutupo wangu. Ndovapeiko amai vangu vagonditendawo? Indeed, when was the last time she had anything to thank Tsitsi for?

Tsitsi would have to make a plan.

What if she could deliver water here to Mbare like they did in Borrowdale and Highlands? No. The people here couldn't afford it. Maybe she could find work in South Africa? Or she could buy eggs and bread in South Africa and sell them here? No. The permit was expensive, and she was afraid of crocodiles. What if she worked at the Reserve Bank, maybe she could find a money printer of her own? No. She knew no one who could give her a job there. What if she got in on dealing? She was intelligent, wasn't she? She could surely grasp the lightning-quick ways of the forex dealers. Or better yet, if she spent money to make money, as they said … but she had none to begin with.

She sighed as she anticipated the questions of their lost expectations. Where is your house? Where did you leave your car? Where did you leave our two-in-one blankets, Chibuku, and the rest of the gifts you are supposed to bring us? Where is the place that you are hiding these things? Where are these things that we were promised when we, although struggling, but nonetheless diligently sent you to the best schools in our reach—with tuck money and groceries? Where are these things, Tsitsi? Where?

For a moment the world around her began to spin. In this dizziness, she made a wish for a benefactor who would show pity on her and give her the money she needed. Even if it was something small, she would be grateful. Just enough for her to breathe. But where would she find such a person? She considered this briefly, before she reprimanded herself for such fairy-tale thinking.

When she started at her job and they had run through her list of duties with her, she wanted to tell them that she held a degree in economics. She soon saw that this would be futile. She and who else? What had she been expecting? she asked herself. All these years safely ensconced behind those university gates, she had had her head so deeply buried in her books that she failed to recognise the changing of the world order beyond those gates. Did she again think that she would be exceptional, not subject to such hardships?

Tsitsi and the rest of the nation who now found themselves degreed and broke, her parents and the parents of the nation with degreed children and still broke, had thought—convinced themselves—that the poverty of their lives could be eliminated by 'professionalisation.'

For months after they had all taken a kombi to see her being capped at the University Athletics Stadium, they had taken to calling her 'Graduate.'

"Graduate, waswera sei?"

"Graduate, we know you are tired from work, but will you please help us read this document?"

"Graduate, what time are you coming back from work?"

Soon it felt like they were mocking her. She felt an irritability that even had her delay or altogether avoid going home to her family.

She thought about Karigo's words again, ndinovapei vagonditendawo? She too wanted to hear her praise name, maita Mukumbudzi! Maita veshungu! The loop played itself over and over in her mind.

Indeed, Tsitsi would have to make a plan so that her mother would have something to thank her for.

Tired of crying, she got up to make supper for herself and Sekuru.

Now, lying in Zvobgo's bed, the memory of that day gave her firm resolution to get up and get on with it.

11

Having firmly resolved that she could not leave her fortunes to fate, Tsitsi stepped timidly into the luxurious dining room of teardrop chandeliers, plush carpets and expensive furniture. She was convinced that everyone had turned to look at her. She felt awkward, conspicuous. Not only would they find her dress too tight, barely able to contain her femininity, her weave distasteful and old, barely hiding the roots of her natural hair, her perfume overpowering yet also barely able to disguise the stench of sweat from her hurried walk from town, but they would wonder too what she was doing at this Party function. But she quickly steeled herself to ignore the imagined looks of the Very Important Persons otherwise preoccupied with Important Things and focus instead on her mission for the night, remembering Chiedza's words not to think too hard about what she was doing and, as she had said in her poor imitation of an American accent, "just go with the flow."

But when she caught sight of Mrs Zvobgo, she immediately lost all of her boldness, her false bravado, and felt the sudden urge to escape the room. She reprimanded herself for making the silly assumption that his wife would not attend. But, no, here she was indeed, in all her imposing glory, in her bright, eye-catching, West African attire, the kind women of the Party had taken to wearing as the de facto uniform of Mothers of the Nation. She was big and stout, and Tsitsi was sure that her shoulders could indeed carry the nation. She had paid attention to her appearance, taking care to apply a layer of a brown-gold lipstick on lined heart-shaped lips. Beautiful diamond studs matched the simple silver watch on her left wrist, earrings and pendant necklace glittering as she talked with, and smiled at, guests. As she waved her hand around, gesticulating in conversation, the diamond ring on her finger caught the light of the chandelier above and sent delicate glints of light across Zvobgo's face. Her breasts were that of a broad matron settled in her years and secure in her marriage. She had the soft pouch of an old wife who had birthed a number of children. Tsitsi imagined that when Zvobgo touched her soft belly, it tormented him and made him feel guilty for his lack of desire.

Mrs Zvobgo had a prominent, regal forehead and deep dimples. She had an air about her, the vanity of one who had been a beauty in her time and still laid claim to the privilege that that had afforded her. Indeed, she had no doubt been the desire of many men and the envy of many women for most of her life. But all of that seemed to have faded now as, Tsitsi could tell, Zvobgo looked at the physicality of his wife dispassionately.

This, of course, was not the first time Tsitsi had set eyes on the woman. Mrs Zvobgo had often come to the office. But this was the first time she had seen the two interact together among their peers. As they stood together greeting other guests, she couldn't help but notice a hint of affection between the two of them. Here and there a hand on his forearm, a palm on the small of her back. Perhaps it was not the affection of passionate lovers, but that kind of familiarity that came about after many years together?

Tsitsi caught Mrs Zvobgo's eye and raised her hand in acknowledgement. The woman's initially blank face betrayed the fact that she had not recognised Tsitsi, but nonetheless, having been in her position for so many years, she was gracious and returned the smile. Tsitsi was offended because, although they had spoken only once in person on one of the many occasions that Mrs Zvobgo had come to see Zvobgo at the office, she had often received instructions over the phone from Mrs Zvobgo, be it to leave a message, remind her husband of an errand, or that her relatives were visiting so he should hurry home. Yet now she did not care to remember her. To her Tsitsi was just hired help, not someone she was obliged to remember.

Nevertheless, Tsitsi decided that she would not allow herself to be distracted by such a small detail and, as planned, seated herself at their table—to what she saw was the surprise for the rest of the table. Other support staff in attendance had been seated at tables at the back of the room, but Tsitsi feigned ignorance of both the seating arrangements and protocol.

Too excitable, or perhaps too drunk to make a fuss, the Very Important Persons let her be. Zvobgo entertained the table with his anecdotes of his urbane life. His hands gesticulated in a manner that told Tsitsi and the rest of his audience that he knew what he was talking about; reinforcing his opinions and illustrating his points. He had the knowledge of the world at his fingertips, reducing impossibly complex matters to basic ideas that even the Mbuya from Dodito could understand.

Despite Mrs Zvobgo's insistence on contradicting him on the details of his anecdotes when she thought there were exaggerations, understatements or misrepresentations, their fellow diners remained firmly in his grasp. They rose and fell with his varied tone of speech, their faces mirroring the ever-changing complexity of his stories. He would pause for effect, bringing them into a precariously controlled silence and then—wha! He would suddenly hit them with the punch line that would bring them into a roar of laughter.

As he talked, waiters walked in and out of the dining room like clockwork toys, taking drinks orders and serving course after course. They wore uniforms that belonged to a time even before that of Smith, Tsitsi was sure, because they bore the insignia of the British crown, which hotel management had not thought to replace since.

"You see, it is quite simple," Zvobgo continued. "What good are a country's resources if they are not for the benefit of the people? It is like a child left with an inheritance, only for it to be enjoyed and squandered by know-it-all estate lawyers or cunning relatives. This doesn't work—we must push toward self-determination."

At this, Mrs Zvobgo laughed. "You see, Zvobgo is really a closet Marxist. He still believes he is some kind of a Salt-of-the-Earth Freedom Fighter. We must all cede moral high ground—from which we have precipitously fallen—to him."

She laughed not with him, for there was no joking now, but rather at him. The kind of direct laugh that told all at the table that she was not afraid of this man. That she, unlike them, was not in awe of him. That this man was an intellectual sparring partner with whom she disagreed on a point. She gave him the kind of laugh that answers a foolish, childish statement. The kind of laugh she imagined an IMF or World Bank official gave when the likes of Zvobgo insisted on their country's sovereignty. This was a serious accusation expressed jocularly.

"My dear," he said calmly, looking into Mrs Zvobgo's eyes, "I would be offended with that Marxist label if I was as beholden to the Washington Consensus as you are." Tsitsi tried to follow—she was, after all, a smart girl, a former distinctions' student. She had knowledge of many of these concepts, but nowhere near the level of detail that Zvobgo now described. "Do you know that it was in the eighties, at the tail end of many of our continent's liberation movements and their victories, that the Structural Adjustment Programmes began? We were independent for five minutes, Guinea-Bissau not even fifteen—"

He stopped to look at Mrs Zvobgo.

"Rudo, why are you shaking your head?"

Rudo. Tsitsi had never heard her addressed as anything but Mrs Zvobgo. A soft name. Love. The woman laughed and shrugged her shoulders.

"What you should be shaking your head at," Zvobgo continued, "is the fact that we lost more of our country's doctors in the early nineties, after the introduction of the Economic Structural Adjustment Programme, than we did when we initiated the Third Chimurenga. Did you know that? It is unfortunate that you believe there is anything there for us when it has done nothing for us as the so-called 'Third World,' except burden us with more godforsaken Structural Government Programmes and sanctions. There is a reason our people used to call them Economic Suicide for African People, and say 'Chenjerai ESAP – Ichamudyai!'"

"Zvobgo, please!" she gave him a light slap on his hand, barely containing her laughter. "I take offence to that—we now go by the term 'developing countries!'"

Tsitsi was annoyed by what she saw as Mrs Zvobgo's insolence. She agreed with Zvobgo's stance and wanted to defend him against his wife. She felt she wanted to say something but had to stop herself from voicing her own arguments. She was well versed in her arguments against neo-liberal economics, and was confident she could take Mrs Zvobgo on. But there was no need, Zvobgo immediately proceeded to lay out his argument and she found herself smiling as he once again won the table over to his side. She took a sip of her wine, which—coupled with Zvobgo's quick retorts—made her feel a little giddy. He spoke to the entire table, but really he was defending himself to Mrs Zvobgo. As his case become stronger, Tsitsi became increasingly excited and eventually decided to jump in to reinforce his words:

"Yes, exactly. Unlike you people," she said, looking directly at Mrs Zvobgo, "who are undecided about your loyalties, we, defenders of our sovereignty, are firmly resolved to do what is best for our people, just as the very same countries who want to impose these neo-liberal policies on us do for their people."

The table fell silent. Immediately she regretted having given in to her impulse, her heady confidence, and simply borne its weight. She pre-empted any response with a smile, hoping to take the bite off her words.

Mrs Zvobgo, however, simply shrugged off her comment, and let her matronly figure fall back into the cushion behind her, where—apparently bored—she combed her manicured fingers into the folds of her gele. Tsitsi was relieved, but still somewhat offended that Mrs Zvobgo had not felt it necessary to respond, like she was not worthy of an argument.

The table rose up in conversation again, reverting to domestic trivialities such as the best places to send their maids and drivers to buy chibage, where to get the least smelly manure and the easiest ways to secure their UK visas. Tsitsi smarted as she busied herself with her cellphone. She read and reread a few gimmicky messages sent by Chiedza:

Dont 4gt dt som lyk it hott! :-)

Releas your inna tyga 2nyt!

Dnt tink 2mch, jst do.

Finally, it was time for the main course. While the rest of the table licked their lips and smiled in gratitude at the platters carried in by the waiters, Mrs Zvobgo leaned forward and, bringing her face to the plate, sniffed the food and scrunched her nose before she gingerly began to eat. Tsitsi found herself surprised that Mrs Zvobgo had been gracious enough to eat, and the more she thought about it, the more irritated she was at this show of ingratitude. Tsitsi saw that Zvobgo was embarrassed too, and shot his wife a reprimanding glance. Mrs Zvobgo looked back at Zvobgo in a way that made it clear she would not be falling over herself for these things. Ha! These things. Things that she easily could have got for herself if Zvobgo had not impregnated her. Either by means of her family's wealth or, if she so chose, by means of her own efforts as a multi-degreed woman. Tsitsi again let out a laugh. A laugh of familiarity, the kind that bred contempt and ingratitude as so brilliantly displayed by Mrs Zvobgo.

Zvobgo was not just anyone, a common man whose wife

could go around making a fool of him. Why did he let her? Maybe he was not the kind of man to make a scene in public and would instead show her when they returned to the privacy of their home. For the rest of the main course, they continued to dominate the table's conversation, speaking to each other in the learnt ways of subtle, biting sarcasm that had steadily, with each year of marriage, displaced the loving sweethearts and sweet-nothings of newlyweds.

By the time the dessert was brought out, their antagonism had dissipated to a more pleasant interaction. They jumped indiscriminately from topic to topic in the way that the Well-To-Do, Well-Heeled, Well-Spoken, Well-Read, Well-Travelled and the Well-Whatever-Was-Good-And-Sophisticated did, forming quite a tag team. Tsitsi had a sense that this show of vibrance and humour to which they had ascended was part of a double act where they only spoke to each other when on stage. Or was this simply a subconscious attempt at rationalising her own intentions? But before she could explore the thought any further, she saw her opportunity when Zvobgo rose from the table and excused himself for the men's room.

"When nature calls, you have to answer," he said, sending the table into another uproar of laughter. The laughter of people high on good deals and good living. Tsitsi wanted to laugh like that too.

"Honestly, I keep telling Tongai to get himself checked," Mrs Zvobgo began once he was out of sight, laughing her terrible laugh again. "Given the number of times he goes to the bathroom a day you would think he has diabetes!"

Tsitsi found herself fighting the urge to get up and slap the woman for undermining him, speaking such indiscretion about such private matters. How could she be speaking so openly—in front of other Very Important Persons, mind you —about his bathroom affairs?

Not only was she indiscreet, she was using his first name when Big Names like his should not be mentioned naked. The woman did not even try to use some sort of endearing term, like Baby or Sweetheart or some other name she surely could have picked up when she had her American lovers as a student in the 1970s. The thought simultaneously incensed Tsitsi and firmed her resolve, giving her a lift off her seat.

Unsure of herself, she slowed her pace as she followed behind him. Then she braced herself to flee back to the dining room, admonishing herself for the foolish assumption that he would be receptive, that he would respond to her, and risk upending his reputation and marriage for the dalliance into which she wanted to entice him.

She thought about how Zvobgo was not an obvious target. He had never made any advances towards her at the office. Nor were there any stories about him, as was usually the case with men of his status. He had always been far too absorbed in his work. She had known his office to have a high turnover of the secretary's position. They had all been girls who would not have hesitated to lie on the office floor if he had asked them to, so they naturally hated working for him because there was no way to advance or gain favours, except by being impossibly efficient in their work. In this case, proximity trumped availability. She wondered if that was a good gamble. What if he dismissed her for indecent behaviour? What would she do then? Then she would really have nothing.

For a moment she stood still, contemplating these facts, but her survival instinct was stronger than her reservations, giving her a sudden surge of urgency. So she continued to follow him until he had to make a left turn into the men's room. Then, suddenly, he stopped and turned around.

"I thought someone was behind me, but I assumed they were going to the ladies.' Is there a problem, Tinashe?"

Her heart beat heavily; she wanted to correct him and tell him that her name was Tsitsi but her throat was dry.

"N-n-no," she began before kicking into character and she reached out and touched his forearm. "It's just that I am sure I could make a better wife."

She said this coyly, in a half-joking tone. She was unsure of herself, surprised at the boldness in her choice of words, and this was the tone that could offer itself as a disclaimer to be used if what she was insinuating was not well received.

He looked at her confused and flustered. She steeled herself to continue, reasoning that there was now nothing to lose. After all, she had got this far, hadn't she?

"I just thought that you might want a little bit more respect from a wife." She chided herself for sounding so scripted, like a movie, but could only continue, now rubbing her hand up and down his arm. Then, as he seemed to be taken aback, she moved in closer to him. He didn't move back. She could smell his wine-tainted breath and felt it quicken.

She locked eyes with him and saw that it was only then that it struck him: her eyes were asking him a question. A sexual one. Then his eyes seemed to question hers in an apologetic, almost embarrassed manner, as if he could not believe that she wanted him. In this moment of realisation, she felt a growing sense of inadequacy on his part. She placed her hand on his chest in a move that was neither ambiguous nor demure, affirming her motives, making it clear that she desired him. Her heart beat heavy with expectation.

Although he said nothing and did nothing to encourage her, she could feel that she was having an effect on him. And that was all she needed to continue. Almost robotically, she took her hand and cupped his balls. She pushed open the bathroom door and led him into a stall. There she unfastened his belt, and knelt on the floor.

She hesitated as she looked at him. The physique of an ageing sportsman. Tall like Taurai ... it was with him that she had last been 'intimate'—if that is what it could be called. If she was unthinking in the moments before this thought of Taurai crept up on her, she now had to work with all her might to continue. It was too late to turn back now. She placed her hands on his thighs to steady herself. She brought her body forward to begin, but found herself short of breath. The thought of Taurai stubbornly lingered.

"St-stop, stop, st—" Zvobgo could barely complete his command before he hooked his hands under her armpits, roughly pulling her up from her knees. The disruption seemed to bring a sense of reality to the unreality they had just momentarily created. He began scrambling furiously for his pants and belt, his shoulder striking her cheek as he bent over.

She let out a yelp, which seemed to make him even more nervous. He grabbed her face searching for bruises or blood, and when he found none, promptly pushed past her.

Confused and with a throbbing headache, she could only think to follow him out of the bathroom. She was startled to find him standing waiting for her.

"H-h-how ... how are you getting home?" he asked quickly, impatiently.

She hesitated, embarrassed. She had actually not thought that far. She certainly couldn't afford a taxi.

"I would have got one of the drivers to take you, but we only have Mrs Zvobgo's driver with us tonight. Here." He handed her a US$100 note.

Tsitsi opened her mouth to say that although she hadn't used taxi cabs often, she was quite sure this was far more than any driver in Harare would charge her, but he stepped in quickly.

"Don't come back to the table, please." He sounded apologetic. "I'll see you at work on Monday." She hesitated, not sure for what. "I'll tell them you had to get the early transport."

Not that they would have noticed. Nonetheless, she took the money and rushed outside, now concerned with not wanting to be seen in her state, a Silly Village Girl, an SRB, who had thought she could seduce such a Made Man, a VIP, and hailed one of the taxis waiting outside the hotel.

If she was honest with herself, she felt a sense of relief. She had been foolish, she knew that. She had taken a chance and it hadn't worked. How could she think that a man of his stature could possibly give it all up for her? Sure, his wife did tend to undermine him, but she could afford to. She didn't need him.

She, Tsitsi, had tried and it hadn't worked. This was the last time.

MONTHS PASSED. Zvobgo, cutting the figure of distant superior, continued as if no such encounter had taken place and she followed suit.

Tsitsi had almost considered telling Mama to try to return kumusha. She would look for someone to help her plough, and, later, harvest. When she was off from work, she would go and help them. If there was any surplus, she could help Mama take it to the market, but really she was most concerned that Mama was fed.

But that would have been silly. It had been years since Baba had died and the house had been taken over. She reprimanded herself for thinking that her relatives would be inclined to be charitable to their sister-in-law and her errant daughter.

Instead, it was Chiedza who helped her. She had been making big, big money, as if she was typing it herself. With that big money she had recently bought herself a new Nissan Navara. She hadn't known how to drive before then, but took to her new car with a shine. The double cab was her only real personal indulgence—instead of moving into the two big houses that she'd bought in Borrowdale and Chisipite after burning money on the black market, she stayed in her Avenues bedsitter flat while renting out the properties.

In addition to those houses, she owned a couple of flats on Samora Machel Drive. She'd complained about the weekly rental payments never being made on time, remarking how much easier it was to get money from the tenants in the bigger houses who, as Chiedza loved to share, "Tapinda, tapinda! Iwe Tsitsi, sometimes these guys want to pay rent for the year—upfront, in cash and in forex! Where have you heard such a thing? Tapinda, tapinda!"

Time was not on Chiedza's side because she still kept her NGO job— "For the contacts," she said— and so seeing an opportunity to 'top-up,' Tsitsi had quickly offered to manage the flats for her. She would get a commission on the rent if she could make sure that she collected it before the end of the first week of the month.

Zvobgo, though, was a demanding boss so she knew she'd be unlikely to get away with the 'jacket on the chair,' so she would go after work—usually on a Friday, when they were let off early from work—and take a brisk walk to the flats before taking a kombi back home. It was a tiring and painful exercise, particularly when the tenants would play truant with her to avoid paying. She found herself coming up with all kinds of carrot-and-stick ploys, such as offering early payment discounts (that would invariably come off her commission), and threatening the children of the house with the police if they didn't find their parents.

Chiedza's 'top-up' wasn't much, but she was nonetheless grateful. It augmented her salary sufficiently enough for there to be a meal for the three of them every night. It bought her some breathing space.

As she made her rounds at the flats she would conjure up her next plan. She had played with the idea of asking Chiedza for a loan to burn some of her own money so she could start her own business. Maybe some flats too? Or perhaps she could go, just leave. Yes, better maybe that she use the money to process the papers for a job in South Africa or Botswana? But she didn't know the first thing about burning money.

Chiedza had tried to explain it to her on several occasions.

"Nhai, Tsitsi, what is so difficult to understand? Weren't you the one who passed economics with a distinction? Burning is just what those textbooks of yours called 'arbitrage.'" Chiedza would wring her hands, "Instead of crying about how useless your Zim dollar salary is, let's burn it and convert them to ma USA, rands or pula—whatever forex suits you. I have a friend, Ruvhi, who works at the bank. She has helped me before—as long as you give her a good cut, she can also help you."

But Tsitsi didn't trust this latest money-making trend, or herself, for that matter. It was high returns for high risk. She had heard a few of the girls in the office talking about their own failed gambles at burning. Not one to be left out, even Sekuru had tried with his pension payout but had got his fingers burnt.

So she decided that she was too risk-averse for all of that. Perhaps she could simply ask Chiedza for a loan to buy a small flat? Nothing too big, even a backroom somewhere in town would do so that she would make decent enough money from the lodgers who would stay there. If not that, she could perhaps start an importing business? Next time the other office girls went to Beitbridge, maybe she could join them and hoard items that were in demand?

THE FIRST TIME that they had attempted anything at the office, she had not known anything would happen until the last moment, because—unskilled and nervous as she was, and skilled and nervous as he was—they had been unable to verbalise anything, let alone a suggestion of any kind of intimacy.

He had summoned her to his office. When she arrived at his door, he said nothing. Because it was late, she had expected that he wanted her to help him pack his briefcase before he left for home. In case he had wanted to dictate something to her, she brought her notebook and pencil. He stood up from his large wooden desk and shut the door behind her. He locked it, too, knowing all the while that it should have remained open.

He approached her, but hesitated briefly, both of them silent and awkward as they stood in such close proximity. Then he pulled her to him. She felt herself dampen at this sudden gesture of authority. The switch aroused her. The touch felt forbidden, and had her wondering whether the fact that she was as youthful as his daughters made it all the more exciting for him. He removed her shirt quickly and decisively, before hastily removing his own. His fingertips traced her nipples, then down to her navel and to the mound of coarse hair between her legs to her womanhood. It had been a while and it felt electric. If she was honest with herself, she was surprised—she had expected that she would have to endure, and not enjoy, the experience. She had at first simply expressed a willingness, with no real desire for him, thinking that was where it would end. But here she was, moving quickly from dampness to wetness, expressing desire for this old man.

She was surprised again when he slapped her bum. A firm slap with a cupped hand that had blood rushing to her cheeks. The conflict she felt was dizzying. She found herself confused, aroused at the sight of his firm legs incongruously lean and sinuous like that of a young man, under his small but firm drum of a stomach. It was a different body from what she had been with in the past, but nonetheless she found herself aroused.

She was surprised, too, that he was not only knowledgeable but caring. She had expected him to be passive and to keel over and sleep when he was done, as the many stories of sex between young nubile women and old perverts dictated.

She thought he would simply hike up her skirt and relieve himself, clothed and standing.

Instead, he was attentive. He showed concern and took pleasure in her pleasure. His stamina impressed her too. It was not that of a young man, certainly. But he was steady. His body was weighty and he grew short of breath. And when the time came, he was visibly annoyed that he was winded and already finished. But Tsitsi was pleased enough. Satisfied. Eager to please, he bent down. For a short time as she felt his tongue deep in her, she wondered if this performance was perhaps thanks to Mrs Zvobgo, whether she had coached him and insisted that he resist his age and continue to be the good lover she must have known in his youth.

When they had finished, she found a sweet sense of satisfaction. It was not because it was passionate, exhilarating lovemaking, but rather because the reality had far exceeded her expectations.

He fell asleep soon on the floor of his office. She lay facing him, with her shoulder in his armpit, their breath intermingling. Her body felt agreeable in his arms.

———

WHEN THEY FINALLY EMERGED, she glowed with the strange sense of confidence. A self-conscious hand tugged at her dress, smoothing creases, while the other flattened her hair.

In his flustered state, he said thank you and gave her money for a taxi cab.

Anyone setting eyes on her inside the taxi would have

thought that this was the life she had always lived. Being picked up or driven alone. She was surprised at how quickly she adapted. But she also harboured the biting sense that she may be pre-empting matters. She nonetheless assumed the impatience of a rich madame. She put on pursed lips, part of the perpetually sour look of disappointment at the efforts of those around her as they consistently fell short of her high standards. They had to know that she too took these things for granted. That she too had high, high standards that could never be met.

Safely on her way home, she fumbled for her phone and texted Chiedza.

12

Their clandestine liaison had quickly become as routine as a loose and simple affair.

But soon that changed. Where she had initially been easy and undemanding, her once-big eyes grew small again, and it became difficult to get them to widen as they had in the past as she grew accustomed to those things their relationship brought with it. She wasn't as excitable. She wanted more. Soon, this desire was voiced. She began to complain to Zvobgo about the state in which she lived. The Catch-Me-If-You-Can electricity. The long, tiring queues at clinics and blah-blah. The alternation between the 100, 010 and 001 meal patterns (where zero means no meal) in an ordinary week; the 101, 110 and 011 in a good week; and the 111 pattern in a week where Zvobgo looked after her. The constant search for distraction for a grumbling stomach that had long since forgotten its last meal. The clothes that did not befit her new, albeit precarious, economic status. And, as he began to give in, she began to rope in Mama and Sekuru into the complaints, sparing no detail.

"Mufunge, Mama nearly collapsed in that queue! Ei! It's so difficult to get the injections for her diabetes!" She was given to embellishments, even of ailments that her mother would have had no way of ever acquiring.

Where would she have got these diseases of comfort when she had only ever lived an austere nun's life for her daughter's sake?

Tsitsi also tried her luck with even bigger demands. So far she had put enough of the money he had given her aside such that she now had the capital she needed to make a considerable amount of money on the black market should he decide that all of this had gone too far.

She imagined him reading her text messages, thinking, This woman is crazy! Can you imagine? You give her a finger, she wants an arm! He would say this as he wrung his hands, making a real show of exasperation.

But yet he obliged.

She could not be sure at what point she had begun to want to stop being the Small House and to live in the Main House. Maybe it had been her natural inclination to ambition, her natural tendency away from complacency. Or perhaps it was when he began to take her into his confidence the first time he brought her to the house, when Mrs Zvobgo had been away at a women's conference overseas.

She wasn't sure what his response would be and braced herself to be chased out of the house. He had already bought her a flat, one that would serve as a love nest of sorts for the two of them.

She tried her luck again.

When they first drove in through the gate onto the gravel driveway to his house, she gasped, taking in the sight. She talked so much, commenting on everything, like an awe-struck villager. Like the SRB she was. She thought about this, but quickly shrugged it off. She was not going to be ashamed that she was not a Born-Location.

It was one of those houses in the leafy suburb of Highlands with a long driveway and a big garden, and a swimming pool and a tennis court and a boma and a boyskai and, and, and.

Inside, almost all the rooms, the many, many of them, had a fireplace. The kitchen countertops and bathroom vanities were granite. The floors were Rhodesian teak. The carpets on top of the Rhodesian teak were of course Persian, dull and boring to the uncultured eye. Stone sculptures by local artists whom Mrs Zvobgo generously patronised were tastefully placed here and there, with a one-of-a-kind Family Under a Tree sculpture—by Henry Munyaradzi, she was later told—boldly welcoming guests into the reception area. Outside of this, the most indulgent piece in the house was perhaps the chandelier in the reception area. Its brilliant bulbous crystals hung low, reflecting sparkling light every which way.

Overall, her assessment of the house was that it may have been impressive in stature, but that she was disappointed by the interior. It was so bare. Lacking in things.

She didn't understand Mrs Zvobgo; she was rich but chose to live, in Tsitsi's opinion, like a pauper. His wife clearly had no interest in buying things. Maybe it was because she had never known poverty. Tsitsi, on the other hand, felt she was well versed in it. Unlike Mrs Zvobgo, Tsitsi wasn't above nouveau riche vulgarities. Not for her any sort of English boarding-school minimalism. She wanted more. She wanted things. Things. Things. Things. Many of them. That much she was willing to admit. She made a private decision then that she would change this when she became the Woman of the House. She knew they said wealth whispered and rich shouted, but what good was having all that they did if she had to keep it hidden like some sort of secret?

When she was younger, it had been the dreams of future prosperity that had kept her awake when the bucket of cold water she kept her feet in could not keep her focused on her studies. And for what? This? No! She had not struggled and strained so much only to have to stinge herself. Neither had Mama. Whoever it was who judged her, let them come and feed and clothe her. Mxm, she snarled like a Scorned Wife in a Nollywood movie—they didn't know her.

There would be heavy silverware. Fish knives for a girl who had eaten with hands and a spoon—and had only learnt to eat with a fork and knife at Mission School. She would have display cabinet upon display cabinet, filled with things. Some things she herself would not know how to use, which of course was not a problem—they would be display cabinets, after all.

Noticing the number of house staff, she thought how, when she had Mama and Sekuru over, she would throw rhetorical questions at them.

"Have I ever told you to be stingy? Do you want our guests to think we don't want them to come again?"

"Jeffreys, is there some kind of shortage in this house? Put out the different drinks for our guests. Bring the glasses and the bucket. Put the ice out also."

So, yes, after a time, this thing that was meant to be temporary was yielding to something more permanent. The comforts of this new life had pushed away many of the objections she would ordinarily have. Things are better already, she thought.

The first time she had complained, she had said that they were for all intents and purposes acting like husband and wife, so why not make it official.

"Zvobgo!" She had dropped the Mister and now used his surname in the way that his colleagues and Mrs Zvobgo did. "Really, how can a man your age be sneaking around in hotels and into his own house? You are too old for this. It's embarrassing—even for me."

"Zvobgo," she said, looking into his eyes as she sucked on his manhood, as if with the intention to drain the blood from his head, "I cannot be a Small House. What will Mama say? What will Sekuru say? I have parents who want an honest woman for a daughter."

She didn't push further, and continued to suck as he lay, silent except for intermittent boyish groans.

Soon enough he capitulated. The first night in the house, she could hardly sleep, even though she had just had a marathon session with Zvobgo. She watched as his chest rose and fell, his parted lips emitting a grumbling snoring rumble from deep within his throat.

It was, of course, not her first time in the house—but actually living in it was entirely different. The vast emptiness around her was unsettling.

She had vast emptiness in her days as well. She was now no longer at the office. She had now made her beauty and upkeep her full-time occupation. She ensured that her hair was always well maintained, the difficulty of which was compounded by the fact that she had now taken up membership at the gym.

She ensured that, even when she went to bed, she was elegant and ladylike. She would only ever be satisfied to slide in under the covers once she had completed her new night-time ritual, as taught by Chiedza, of dabbing on face cream, which in turn led to her face acquiring a 'soft, dewy glow,' or so the label had proclaimed. Of course, she could no longer wear old stockings on her head to keep her hair in place as she slept. Now she wore a beautiful silk scarf. When she woke she ensured that the time spent unbathed and without make-up was minimal. She had initially tried waking before Zvobgo so that she would have her face made up by the time he rose, but found it difficult to beat him because he woke at an ungodly 4 a.m. for his morning runs.

For a long time she remained inefficient in her newly acquired beauty routine. Make-up was her weak point. Of course, she was helped by the constant reminders and tutorials that Chiedza gave.

"Ko chiiko, Tsitsi? Can't you see that you can't mix those colours? Zvikaramba zvakadai we'll have to swap and I will have to be the Small House!"

"Shamaz, that's not how you do it! How many times did I show you this tichiri kuSwinton? It's like you are a child at crèche! How can your hand be so unsteady?"

"Tsitsi! Don't close your eyes when you put on mascara, or you'll keep staining your face and everyone will think Zvobgo beats his Small House!"

These were Chiedza's common refrains as she feigned annoyance. In fact, Tsitsi sometimes took longer than necessary and purposefully fumbled, because she knew that her dear friend relished giving the lessons.

Nonetheless, her routine was quite taxing. The constant

glances in the mirror, the endless retouches. She found herself with newfound respect for the women she had looked down upon in the past, and she persevered until her hand became steady and she learnt which colours worked well together on her dark skin tone. It was like learning a new craft. Studying a new subject.

But with this preoccupation, she became passive as far as the maintenance of the house was concerned. Lazy, is what her mother would have called it had she seen her behaviour. Mama had always said that the woman of a household never learns the meaning of 'sit.' Tapinda muchirungu, Sekuru would have said. Tsitsi now had her meals served to her. The skin on her hands became soft and she was almost sure that she could feel herself losing some of the strength in them. She never so much as rinsed a plate or cup. She left her dirty plates and cups wherever she finished using them, in the kitchen, lounge and even the bedroom. She left clothes wherever she undressed. She could do this; there were many house girls and boys. And God forbid she return to a room to find the items she had left still there. When she spilt something or broke a glass, she didn't leave the spot in search of a mop or broom, she left in search of one of the many servants in the house.

She sensed, however, that this may have been excessive, beyond simple laziness. That even Mrs Zvobgo—though she would not go as far as washing dishes or sweeping the floor herself—would at least put the plates in the sink, pick up the clothes. Zvobgo, from what she could tell, did not mind, as long as he returned to a clean house. As a result, she was relieved, absolved from the guilt and awkwardness that threatened to unbalance her.

She settled in faster than she had expected. In fact, the

transition seemed so seamless that she wondered if it raised suspicions that her actions had long been premeditated and that this was now simply an execution of her meticulous plans.

She sent the clothes that had been left by Mrs Zvobgo with a driver to a women's refuge in town. She felt she couldn't be so disrespectful as to distribute them among the household staff. Imagine them meeting Mrs Zvobgo in town wearing one of her outfits? No. Nor could she stand to see that from any members of her own family.

The photographs that had remained she also removed. Of course, she could not keep them in the house—an unnecessary memento of his old life. She thought it too cruel to destroy the pictures, and even considered mailing them to Mrs Zvobgo, but thought better of it and in the end sent them to be stored in the room behind the garage.

One of the pictures lingered in her mind, however. Mrs Zvobgo, a young woman with a nubile body, fresh faced, framed with a neatly maintained Afro. In this picture Zvobgo leaned on her, his head resting on his hands on her shoulder. The two were not looking into the camera, but appeared to be in mid-conversation. It was a candid photo, perhaps taken by a friend who, seeing the sense of serenity and oneness between them, had been inspired to capture the moment. In it they looked like true companions.

There was another picture too. An older Zvobgo and Mrs Zvobgo on their wedding day. He wore white gloves that stood out against his black wedding suit and sported a white rose on the lapel of the jacket. His hair in a side parting. Mrs Zvobgo was wearing a long, trailing veil. It was pulled back to reveal her straightened hair, with wedding rice scattered all over it. She wore a simple white dress with sleeves. Her hands in white lace gloves, holding a bouquet of roses. Here they stood with their small bridal party outside a small church. Again, a candid photo. Mrs Zvobgo was gesturing for Zvobgo to come closer and, as he obliged, was captured mid-step.

Tsitsi couldn't help but sense that Zvobgo was now a different man from the one in the photos. She wondered about the type of pictures that would be taken of her with Zvobgo. The ones that had already been taken had been formal. All of them calculated and posed.

She was aware of the great distance between her and Zvobgo, a great gulf of life experience. A man who had had children, a wife, a partner he had loved and betrayed. She had had a boyfriend or two, yes, but nothing serious.

He was some decades ahead of her. Of a different generation. A different sensibility. He was often amused by what she said, and would smile the indulgent smile of a parent listening to the naïve proclamations of his offspring.

It was not that he saw her as a child. There was just an avuncular air about his treatment of her. In truth, despite her education, she sometimes felt out of her depth in conversations with him. In her vague imaginations of a husband of a young woman, she had imagined a man who knew more than her. So, in that way, hers was not so much of a need of adjustment of the reality against the expectation, as she had so often had to do all her life.

He seldom solicited her opinion outside of domestic matters. If he did, it was more as a form of entertainment than for any meaningful counsel.

"Young lady," he would say gravely, with his best professor's voice, "I give up, you have challenged me. I deserve the respect of your attention as I dare to defend myself against what I see as a spurious argument."

Tsitsi was at times offended by this. It sometimes annoyed her that he did not show real interest in her apart from the domestic and coital. She sometimes felt as if she were little more than a pliant machine whose use was fucking and flattering him.

But before she could get carried away and act on this anger, she would pull herself back, aware that it was probably best for all concerned for her to remain as far removed from comparisons with Mrs Zvobgo as possible. She often found herself having to draw back to maintain a version of the deference she had adopted when she was his secretary. Entertaining him with her sometimes questioning, youthful attitude, playfully opposing him, but always careful to stay away from the position of intellectual equal.

One day she heard him on the phone with one of his daughters, with whom he had reconciled. As he spoke, she thought of her own father. He was not someone she would think of much. He had been dead for so long, it had seemed that was all she remembered him to be—gone. That memory of gone-ness had almost entirely displaced the memory of the presence of the God-fearing man who had been very proud of his singular wife and daughter.

The God-fearing man, with no time for the superstitions of his brothers. He had told them repeatedly, in no uncertain terms, that he would not have any of it in his household.

The God-fearing man who believed that his lot in life was God's plan.

The God-fearing man who had met his helpmate at the Bonda Mission. For her beauty (specifically, her dark skin, which—oddly, in the eyes of others—he thought fit to complement his light skin, which had allowed him kutamba Chikaradhi as a young man before he had discovered God and gained some pride in himself as an African man) and her demure nature (particularly, her self-effacing ways), he had plucked her from the mission grounds and taken her kumusha, which was kwaChihera.

The God-fearing man and loving father who, on his teacher's leave, would dutifully bring books for his daughter. When Tsitsi was not yet of school-going age, he had religiously taken her through the a-e-i-o-u, sa-se-si-so-su, sva-sve-svi-svo-svu, tsa-tse-tsi-tso-tsu (his favourite) of Pindura 1, 2 and 3. This was before she could read on her own. To his delight, she would make a show of reading the travails of Farai, Sekai et al, models for their obedience and responsibility because, as it were, "Sekai musikana akanaka. Sekai anoita basa rake ne simba, anoita achipedza. Sekai anofarira vabereki vake. Mwana ano dadisa."

Tsitsi's eagerness to read to her father had lasted until she had begun to grow dubious of their ability to smile and work hard through all household tasks given to them by Baba and Amai, and sometimes Mbuya and their neighbour, vaHera. Her dubiousness was at its height when they smiled through what Tsitsi hated to do most, which—as the only child in the house—was to herd cattle with other children, mostly boys, from the village.

Seeing her loss of interest, her father had graduated her to longer books and gifted her with his very own copies of Runako Munjodzi, Kunyarara Hakusi Kutaura? and A Storm is Brewing, which had kept her preoccupied for the rest of primary school and into secondary school as she struggled with Rungano's words, not only for their English, but also for their double and sometimes triple meanings. Her father's copies were ones she'd loved—for their dog ears and ballpoint scratchings under words, or sometimes phrases, sentences and entire paragraphs that told her what he thought remarkable, perhaps a surprising twist, a proverb, a new word he hadn't heard before, an old word he had last heard on the lips of his grandparents or a brilliant articulation of one of life's strange phenomena. She too would underline what she deemed noteworthy, beginning an unspoken kinship that she hoped her own child would discover one day. A conversation between three generations.

Soon after he had died, his memory too painful to be kept present, she threw her copies away.

ZVOBGO, the father, now remarked to his daughter that his 'harem of women' had left him, and offered a gentle laugh. It sounded as if she had laughed too before putting her mother on the phone. He spoke with a kind of familiarity that caused Tsitsi to feel a sense of resentment. To her mind, she had driven them apart in physical distance, but they nonetheless seemed tied to one another by the physical manifestations of the consummation of their marriage.

If Tsitsi were honest, she had been surprised by the relative ease of it all.

Chiedza had been surprised too. "Chokwadi ndechekuti Mrs Zvobgo is definitely a better woman than I am. I always say, if an 'unclassy' situation happens to me, then I reserve the right to 'unclassy' actions—petrol, matchsticks and all."

A woman like Mrs Zvobgo, one of such stature, with such a name, to divorce so easily? Chiedza had read in the papers that she had been the one to have filed the papers. That he had been the one to initially refuse to give his signature. That she had threatened him if he didn't. With what, Tsitsi didn't know.

Zvobgo had not spoken to her of this. He had made it seem as if it were all his choice. His choice to begin taking care of her family. His choice to promote her from the status of the Small House. His choice to have her become the Woman of His House.

His choice to endure the initial disapproving and disparaging looks. She saw their looks.

"But, Zvobgo," they said, "you are not the first to have a Small House. We have our own, but we don't go and chase out our wives, the mothers of our children, in order to put these Small Houses in the Main House. If you really didn't want to have to continue playing truant with your wife, why didn't you just make the young girl your second wife?"

Their eyes would ask until they would later be duly informed that Mrs Zvobgo would not have any of it. To which they would respond that it was perhaps because she had been spoilt by the fact that he, a man of his stature, had been so good before.

To which the informant would have a hearty chuckle. To which the other would in turn respond: Besides was it not her degrees that had gone to her head?

To which the other would answer: I think it's the kind of family she came from. Very proud, vaivhaira. Her father used to own businesses in Chitungwiza. He also had the Tingamara Buses all those years. He sent all of his children, all girls, to school. Primary school right up until university. All of those girls.

To which the other would question: Was she not part of those Party women who made a noise about having to wombera and welcome the men ministers at the airport as they returned from overseas visits?

To which the other would respond: No? But in any case, wasn't she supposed to become the Minister of Women Affairs, Gender, Community Development and All Things Considered UnImportant in the Greater Scheme of Things when there was that fall out with the first minister?

To which the other would confirm: Yes, that was before her arrogance got in her way and she caused some trouble in the department. Very arrogant woman that. Yes, even during the Chimurenga we warned against that sort of bourgeois imperialist feminism, women's lib what-what of hers.

To which they would then both agree: With all of this to have had to put up with, perhaps it was understandable that the old man had put the Small House in the Main House. Poor old man.

In no time, they agreed, they would have a child and all would be forgotten.

Eventually, Tsitsi believed, it all had become his choice, although at times she would find him looking at old pictures of the two of them (the ones she would eventually throw out) and, at times when he was particularly forgetful, he would call her Rudo. But that was not grounds to be unhappy with the relationship. As long as he was there. He was there and providing. She could accept the situation.

She could accept the situation—whereas Mrs Zvobgo could not.

Mrs Zvobgo was not an Undivorceable Woman. Not an Undivorceable Woman, who would refuse to see that she was no longer wanted. That he had a new life.

No, she was not an Undivorceable Woman who would

defiantly continue to wear her wedding ring. Continue to wear hers, even when he had long since stopped wearing his.

No, she was not an Undivorceable Woman who could forgive a husband's sins for the sake of a name. A name that was revered for its bravery in the Second and Third Chimurengas.

No, she was not an Undivorceable Woman who could forgive a husband's sins (of the flesh and others) for the sake of sanctity. The sanctity of a holy union.

No, she was not an Undivorceable Woman who could forgive a husband's sins for the sake of family. For the sake of a family that would, too, have its fair share of its own open secrets—children in the bush, incest, Small Houses, bruised bodies and the like.

No, she was not an Undivorceable Woman who would appeal to his family—first to Tete and then his brothers and, if alive, the mother, who in this case was not. Appeal to his family so that they in turn would appeal to their dear, but misguided, brother, son.

No, she was not an Undivorceable Woman who could bring out dockets of her years as a good muroora to the family. A good muroora who was always hardworking and, very importantly, humble. A good muroora who had dutifully looked after their sick mother before she had died.

A good muroora who had been a mother to all his siblings —and the many other relatives—who had needed a halfway house of sorts when they had come to town from the village.

No, she was not an Undivorceable Woman, who was going to produce any dockets in public either. No dockets that contained details of the many properties acquired through impropriety at his job.

No, she was not an Undivorceable Woman.

The ex-Mrs Zvobgo, Ms Rudo Tingamira, was in fact a Very Divorceable Woman.

Yes, she was in fact a Very Divorceable Woman who took off her wedding ring and, in turn, had her ex-husband Mr Zvobgo, the almost Undivoreceable Man had it not been for her Divorceable-ness, discover just how Divorceable he was.

13

He called her baby sometimes. Baby girl even. Darling. Sweetheart. Sweetie-pie. The sweet nothings that felt incongruous among the vast vocabulary that dropped from his lips. She wondered if he wasn't trying too hard to be young and hip.

It wasn't as if he did not see the looks from others. He had just never addressed them, and so she did not address them either. To be sure, neither of them had addressed the looks directly. Tsitsi had begun with her matching geles and African attire, approximating a younger Mrs Zvobgo. Zvobgo in turn encouraged them and began making a point to take her along to more official events.

As they arrived, he would place his hand at the base of her neck, or her lower back, his fingers seeking its warmth. She was grateful to have arrived with him. Without him, she felt like everyone looked through her. Judging her, not as the apparent cause of the breakdown of a decades-long marriage, but rather for her class. They took her in, and then switched between him and her, searching for the link.

"This is my partner," he would say.

Someone had once remarked that that sounded very French. She wasn't sure what that meant. She was just grateful not to be called a girlfriend or Small House.

Grateful that, despite the scepticism, they were greeted and regarded as one entity, even if only temporarily in their eyes. When they separated, she to the other women, he to the other men, she felt she had been thrown into the deep end, feeling the strain of having to make small talk with these women.

Sometimes, when the genuinely ignorant and genuinely spiteful alike would proudly announce themselves and their attachments to their powerful husbands, with "Ndinonzi Mai Nhingi," or for the ones particularly tickled by their husbands' professions, "Ndinonzi Mai Musoja", in expectation that she too would legitimise her presence, she would defiantly answer, "Ndinonzi Mai Zvobgo."

Even through this domestic sizing up, in between talk of the best pressure cooker brands to be found in Johannesburg and the best tailors for the many swathes of machira picked up in Kuala Lumpur, she was buoyed by the knowledge that her presence would again be ratified when she left with him.

There was no powerful, superlative emotion attached to him. Theirs was not a passionate love. In fact, Tsitsi had never really thought of that word in the context of their relationship. His commitment to looking after her and her family was all that she had really, all that she had considered. If she really needed to use that word, which she didn't, it would surely describe his actions, if not their emotional connection. In that way, hers was the love of gratitude she felt for a man who endeavoured to look after her and her family. Perhaps the dormant love for a father was now awakened and he was now the object of it.

One of the benefits of an older man, as she and Chiedza had now so often discussed, was that he was his own agent. As a rule, there were three people in a marriage. Man, wife and mother-in-law. Here there was no mother-in-law. He was an old man and his mother was long dead. And there was no mother or any other authority in his life from whom Tsitsi had to seek approval. No mother-in-law to endear herself to. No one to calculate the right time to begin to call 'Mama' or risk being seen as too forward. No one to send gifts of clothes or food or household trinkets or such things to fill the house her son had dutifully built her. No one to put on a show of domesticity when she came to visit their home. No mother-in-law to talk to Zvobgo in roundabout ways about how incompetent she may have been in running the household and taking care of her son. She only had to contend with that when it came from her own conscience.

For that matter, nor was there a father-in-law to dissuade him from his new choice in women. No father-in-law with a roving eye and whose sexual solicitations she had to pretend not to hear. Yes, some of his mother's sisters were still alive, but none of them had the authority to intervene in his domestic matters.

That meant there was greater freedom for Tsitsi to find her own rhythm within the household.

No in-laws to balk at the fact that their traditional marriage had not been ratified by the birth of grandchildren. No in-laws to insist that he demand his cattle and take her back to her family home. No one to discourage plans of the white wedding. There was no external party to do this. Only Zvobgo would be the one to do that.

14

She thought about how she had been taught in church to put others before herself. This is what her mother preached. This is what her mother did. This is what Tsitsi had been taught. That is what she was doing now. She was doing this for them. It was not for her own good.

But what if, one day, they were not there? What if they died? She'd imagined Mama and Sekuru in an accident. Some kind of holy one where they felt no pain, but would nonetheless be taken. Then she would not have to do this.

But she didn't really want that. Then she would have no reason to give herself to Zvobgo. She shuddered at the thought. If she was honest, it was not so much because of the thought of losing them, but rather losing this new life.

No. No. She was firm again. She could not begin to regret her decisions now. This entire situation had been forced on her unwilling spirit.

The torment of the idea pushed her out of her bed and to her mother's house. Perhaps it was the pull to redeem herself by showing her dutifulness that got her on the road to Kuwadzana.

Ndapota! Vharai Gedhi! said the sign on the gate that her mother had had painted when the house had been rebuilt. Tsitsi hooted and Susan quickly came running.

She went into the house without bothering to greet the girl.

She found Mama seated alone, and felt her heart slowly tense as she realised that Sekuru was not around. She chastised herself, too, for ignoring Susan and not asking whether Sekuru, the faithful placeholder he was, was there.

"Makadii, Mama?" she asked in the middle of an awkward embrace.

It was not that she wanted to speak to Mama; she just wanted to be in her presence. A presence from which she could sieve unspoken maternal reassurance, separating it from the mounds of silent judgement.

Mama sat in her rigid dignity. She was accustomed to the dignity of poverty and grief. Even when she had been relieved of her hardships, hers had been a way of life long formed, and she showed no desire to change. She seemed to have no unwillingness to go to the grave. In fact, there was an unsettling sense of her willingness, despite her relative youth, to be pulled to the other side where she would be free of all worldly concerns.

She gave a slow, subdued growl as if there were things that were knocking at her chest, demanding to be let out.

Tsitsi remembered how Mama had always tied her zambia tight around her stomach as a means of suppressing distracting urges and emotions. A means to simultaneously muffle her body's cries of hunger and suppress the flames of anger before they left her heated belly.

The grief of widowhood, of losing a husband and only to be harassed by his brothers, remained pressed on her.

The flatness of eyes told of an owner who had decided not to say anything or voice any further judgement. Accepting and unquestioning in a way that nonetheless still seemed to thrust judgement and accusation on her daughter. Whether knowing or not, she had woven an invisible net of guilt and an unpaid debt of gratitude that she felt she could not escape. From the time Tsitsi had begun to speak of this Zvobgo of hers, Mama had refrained from making any sort of comment, but yet it remained obvious that she took a dim view of Tsitsi's actions.

Tsitsi knew that this was in keeping with her and the Women's Guild's endeavours to exhibit the virtues followed by Mary: simplicity, silence, solitude and surrender.

She sensed her mother's life to be one in perpetual postponement. Simplicity and frugality in order to assure Tsitsi's future, which had now come but had not yet brought an end to that way of life.

With each silence she thought of Kunyarara Hakusi Kutaura? Each time she did, she found herself thinking that she would much prefer Mama's words.

She had spoken initially.

Sharp, heavy words.

The heaviest one came bouldering out the day Tsitsi had brought Zvobgo home. Although Mama had known him, as everyone did, it was really that she knew of him. Confronted by his physical presence, his age, the word pushed itself angrily out of her mouth, needing to be said and find itself heard by all concerned.

"Hure."

Said angrily and yet with a soft deliberation. Whore. Prostitute. In some places, chimbwido.

That was the first and last time Zvobgo had come to visit. Tsitsi stayed away for weeks, perhaps a month. In that time she had nonetheless continued to ensure their upkeep.

In that time Mama had found new words for it. Mhepo, she had called it. Mhepo yakaipa. A terrible wind that would surely pass if she appealed in prayer to God. God, the very God who, despite his seeming neglect, if not disdain, for the three quarters left behind by the one quarter, would surely answer. Mhepo yakaipa. Moyo wakasvipa. God would answer with its opposite force, moyochena.

She had said to her brother Dickson with such certainty, "Mhepo ichaenda."

But the wind did not pass. Instead, it seemed to grow stronger, gaining steadily as its force pulled them each in successively. First Tsitsi, then Dickson, before it had succeeded in sweeping her up in its gust. Powerless against this wind, she had withdrawn into her silence. A silence that spoke of shame. Of failure. Of capitulation. Of complicity. The worst.

Since then she had never spoken a word against Zvobgo. Nor did she speak or ask of him or of any of the details of Tsitsi's life in sin with him.

Tsitsi had wondered if this had meant Mama had surrendered? Was this what was meant when the Women's Guild members had been taught to be able to say "fiat" in all of life's circumstances: "Let it be done unto me"?

"Mwanangu." The gentleness in her tone pierced Tsitsi's heart. My child. The words appeared to soften her features. Tsitsi found herself staring at her mother. Zvisineyi, the second of two children born to Ndaipaneyi, the second of

Onisimo's three wives. Zvisineyi, raised poor in the mission, one of two children in the household who had the fortune of finding Fata's favour. The favour that had seen her through secondary school and a teaching diploma.

Maybe Tsitsi imposed too much on her mother, expected too much? Maybe the picture of her as unwavering was inaccurate, unfair even?

"Ndakuenda kuchechi, if I don't leave now, I'll be late for mass."

"Mama, I'm here. I'll take you. Mungafambe ndiripo here?"

She didn't resist.

Tsitsi held her as she negotiated the Land Cruiser's step and climbed onto the passenger seat. She felt some sense of fulfilment and redemption in being able to do this for her mother. She thought again of Karikoga's words. She too wanted to hear her praise name.

Whether or not Mama could allow herself to acknowledge it, Tsitsi knew she had given her something to thank her for.

She remembered the two of them carrying her school trunk from their house to the bus stop some three kilometres away. The trunk would float askew between them, the handles held at different heights, higher on Mama's side. Mama was always simultaneously indignant and incredulous at the cruelty of those who sped past them ferrying one, maybe two passengers and yet ignoring their hitchhikers' signs, instead spraying dust in their faces.

"Ndo hunonzi hutsinye!"

The hurt and bitterness in her voice even more palpable on days when it would rain.

On one occasion, it had rained sheets, with biblical grandeur. That day the cruelty of those motorists had wavered; some had been careful to negotiate the road in such a manner that ensured that they did not splash mud onto the luckless pedestrians negotiating the sodden dust road, and one was so kind as to stop and offer them a lift. On seeing the red taillights of the truck, they had merely moved aside, thinking that the driver had stopped to check something on the vehicle, perhaps a wheel damaged by an unseen rock or unanticipated pothole. They were indeed surprised when, after moving the logs and bags in the back of the truck to one side, he called for them. His colleague quickly alighted and helped him to lift the trunk into the back. He apologised for his meagre offering of a blanket they could use to cover themselves, saying that although they would still get wet, they at least would get to their destination sooner.

"Mazvita, mazvita—bless you, children of God," Mama had said, as the rain mixed with the tears running down her cheeks.

***

"I'll wait for you, until you are finished at church," Tsitsi said as she helped Mama alight from the vehicle.

She had nowhere to go. She was not in the mood to see Chiedza, nor did she want to return to the house to be further tormented, as she imagined, by Zvobga's house staff for the fact that she had no claim to it.

The priest, Fata Gombo, would be brusque in his delivery. Straight to the point. The way she had always liked her sermons to be. She retained some of her mother's conservative sensibilities and in that way had retained the sense of the moral superiority of the Catholic Church, and even the other established denominations, such as the Anglicans and Methodists, for their bare-to-bones, formulaic delivery of the Lord's word. No room for deviations, embellishments or liberal interpretations. So she knew it would be short.

That Mama did not ask her to come in endeared her even further to Tsitsi. As she waited, she had the thought that she might go inside for a confession.

At the entrance, she found herself hesitating. She had not been to church for so long. She found it hauntingly silent, but as she began to make her way inside, her ears adjusted and she could make out the gentle murmur of prayers.

"Hail Mary, full of grace ..."

"... Conceived without sin."

"Without sin, my child."

Quietly, she slipped into the confessional.

Sign of the Cross.

"Fata Marwira, I don't know how to say this."

"Yes, my child, it is all right to speak. This is the House of the Lord."

She hesitated. "Thank you, Fata." She hesitated again. "Fata, if a sin is committed selflessly, is it really still a sin?"

Surely it could not be judged with the same weight of other self-serving sins? It was like a white lie, only spoken for the good of others. This was an act committed for the good of others, was it not? Yes, that was what it was, so judgement would surely have to be suspended, or at the very least, be lessened.

"My child, what is it that you wish to confess?" he prodded patiently.

I'm asking on behalf of a troubled friend of mine. That was what she wanted to say, but knew it was a futile disclaimer to a man whose ears had surely been assailed with far worse.

"F-f-f-ata," she insisted, "Fata, I know I would not do it if my own security was my only concern."

She said it with the sincerity of an unwilling mineworker lamenting his labour in a faraway Johannesburg, trapped in a dark, humid inferno for the good of the faithful wife and five children he had left back home in the countryside.

Fata sighed and spoke with learnt patience, "Don't be ashamed with me in the room here with you. I am just God's messenger. Merely a conduit. Only He can judge."

Somehow she felt less than comforted by those words. She began to feel silly. This was a futile attempt at redemption, a way to avoid judgement. She cleared her throat as if about to speak, but instead she remained silent.

Eventually, well accustomed to such dances with guilty parishioners, Fata offered, "Pray, my child. Prayer is the surest route to heaven."

His instruction made her uneasy. She couldn't bring herself to communicate with God directly; she had been hoping that the priest would intercede on her behalf.

"Fata, please," she pleaded. "I have not been able to come to the House of the Lord because of this."

"Yours must be a terrible sin if it has caused you to stay away from the House of the Lord for so long. What is it?" His voice had lost some of its patience. Hearing no response, he repeated, "Prayer is the surest route to salvation."

"Father," she paused for some time before continuing. She

stumbled over her words, ashamed, wondering how she would confess her sins. "Fata," she said, "I cannot pray."

"Well then how can I help you?" he asked, almost laughing. He sounded incredulous and she imagined him shaking his head. "How can you ever hope to receive if you don't voice your desires to the One who makes them possible? You know the scripture: ask and ye shall receive."

How wonderful the world would be if it were that simple, she thought to herself. She got up. No, Fata could not help her.

"Of course. You are right. Thank you for your time, Fata. I now have direction."

"I thought you had a confession?"

"Yes, yes. I will pray about it and then I will return to you."

"Take care then. God bless you, my child."

His blessing remained ringing in the air, unanswered.

WHEN SHE GOT HOME after dropping Mama off, she greeted none of the house staff she encountered. She simply passed them and locked herself in the bedroom.

She knelt at the base of their bed and clasped her fingers in gesture for prayer. If she could not do it in Fata Marwira's judgemental presence, perhaps she could do it on her own, in her own space.

"Mwari Baba," she began, aloud as if that would reinforce the message, but soon paused, not finding the words to continue. She thought of how she needed her God and felt her heart begin to thump hard with her pressing desire.

"Mwari Baba ..." she began again. Still no words as her

heart beat even faster. She bit her lip and began to cry. She wept for some time, thinking about the precariousness of her situation. There was always a sense of this. It had been temporarily relieved when Zvobgo had signed the divorce papers, in which Mrs Zvobgo cited 'irreconcilable differences.'

There were no children to fight over. His two daughters were now women with their own households, married—to white men, it was rumoured—and living abroad in Malaysia. There was no property to fight over either. Mrs Zvobgo didn't want the house. It was stained, she said. She couldn't stand to sleep in the same bed Zvobgo had used with his mistress. She had come up with an inventory of vehicles (sedans, 4x4s, tractors), properties (stands, flats, houses, plots, farms) and businesses (butcheries, estate agents, importers) to which the entire country would have become privy. She did this not because she wanted the property, but simply as a means to frustrate her errant husband. Once she had achieved that, she was content to move on.

She only asked that she be afforded the same allowance as she had enjoyed as his wife so that she could start over with peace of mind.

This had unsettled Tsitsi. A benign strand of doubt that had grown into something bigger and more malignant. She had seen that Mrs Zvobgo's dignity in this otherwise humiliating affair had been somewhat endearing to Zvobgo. As a result, she had always felt a little insecure, uncomfortable, vulnerable even. As far as she had known, he had never been a promiscuous man. She had been the one to break him into this world. His pursuits now would surely be indiscriminate as he found it easier to slip in and out of thighs.

Soon she was back to square one. Back to her insecurities, insecurities that grew more and more as Zvobgo avoided taking the next step in further cementing their relationship.

On the insistence of her mother, Zvobgo had paid roora. Or rather, to be sure, it was on the insistence of a delegation of her father's brothers led by Babamukuru Edzai, who in turn had caught wind of their Long Lost Daughter's affair with Zvobgo, the Very Important Person, and decided to climb onto a bus to Harare and demand what was due to them.

Much to Tsitsi's anger and Zvobgo's embarrassment, the Babamukuru Edzai delegation of uncles camped outside the Ministry where Tsitsi worked, saying, "Hatina mwana anoita zvekubika mapoto nemurume!"

Sekuru had initially objected to their presumptuousness. However, in keeping with her values as a faithful Women's Guild member and her desire to vindicate herself as a good muroora, despite their ill treatment of her when their brother had died, Mama had simply said, "It's the right thing to do pachivanhu chedu."

Wanting to contain the embarrassment of the rural band's squatting campaign to his Ministry, Zvobgo had quickly arranged for negotiations to take place that very weekend.

As they had settled on receiving a fridge and other such smaller items in lieu of mombe yaamai, Sekuru Dickson had uttered, much to Mama's disapproval, "Honai! Remember when you chased away my sister? And now you want to share in what we have achieved."

Despite her resentment of her uncles, Tsitsi had been grateful for the brief sense of security that it had brought her.

Now, as the uncertainty around her felt as if it were

closing in on her as empty shelves became emptier, long queues became longer and quadruple zeroes of the currency quadrupled, it was not enough.

It was not enough.

She suddenly got up off her knees, and wiped her tears. But the tears continued to fall as she rummaged through her cupboard until she found her old prayer book. Then she returned to her kneeling position, holding the blue leather-bound book in her hands.

"Our Father, who art in heaven, hallowed be Thy name …" she felt as if the words had been written for her. She would not have to think of how to approach God, the script was already there. "… Forever and ever. Amen."

With those last words, a sense of relief descended on her. Through her recital of the Lord's Prayer, God would surely see her actions and hear her desires. She could now leave it in His hands.

15

How could she be so foolish as to expect results so quickly?

It had been less than a week since she had knelt down and prayed. After all, God worked in His own mysterious ways, did He not? Who was she to be so prescriptive about when and how? She herself couldn't even say what she wanted or expected. Was it that she simply wanted him to call her baby and sweetheart again? For him to notice what she wore? Or was it more? What would make her feel secure?

She grew impatient when he continued in the same vein, barely taking note of her and dismissing her when he did. She couldn't remember the last time they had eaten a meal together.

While other leaders grew prosperous stomachs and spent their time in useless discussions, Zvobgo threw himself even further into work. He crossed the country, north and south, in a non-stop campaign with a vigour that belied his age. That vigour saw him taking to battle in beerhalls, stadiums, lecture halls, conferences and private dining rooms.

Tsitsi decided to reinforce her plea by fasting. Yes, fasting. It was what Mama held to be the most potent weapon of faith. It wasn't Lent, but she was desperate. She was sure this could be understood.

She was grateful, though, that Zvobgo was not around; she could only imagine his response. "Are you dieting now?" clearly irritated at this seemingly frivolous water-only indulgence of hers.

The lack of nourishment sharpened her senses and she suddenly seemed to perceive more. Her eyes saw more. Her ears saw more. Her heart felt more.

She bowed her head down and attempted to pray again. Down, in infinite fear of, and shame in, her actions.

Lord, how am I contradicting you? You clearly understand that I must? she wanted to ask.

Yes. Surely He must understand that self-evident fact.

She started off well enough, adjusting to the feeling of her limbs as perpetually light and agile. However, by the third day of the fast, the only way she could keep from capitulating to her hunger was to sleep. When she was awake, she was too feeble to do anything and found herself in a perpetual daze.

She couldn't believe how weak she had become. Depriving herself was nothing new, of course. She had often fasted before exams and whenever Mama had asked her to join her. And of course, she had long been used to alternating 100, 010, 001, 110, 011 and 110 meal plans so this shouldn't have been much of a strain.

The house staff clearly found it amusing that she was apparently starving herself, presumably in an effort to become slimmer—the way young madams often did. She saw this in the way they continued to ask her if they should prepare meals, despite her repeated instructions not to.

And then, at the end of the fourth day, she fainted.

When she came to, she opened her eyes to the figure of Mary, the house girl, standing over her. She stood helpless, fretting over what to do with the fallen madam.

Still dazed and delirious, Tsitsi's thoughts drifted to her last indulgence, savings spent on her most lucrative investment. She remembered the four parts. First, there was the twelve-inch weave that preyed on her receding hairline. Second, were three mock-satin bra-and-panty sets from the bundle Mai Shava had brought from her last trip to South Africa. Third, the abnormally high gogos that had made her reel from pain after walking to work on the days she couldn't afford to catch a kombi. Fourth, the lightening cream that had cemented her new look.

Looking at herself in the broken mirror on the peeling wall of the room she shared with her mother, Tsitsi was slightly unnerved. She stood in front of the mirror, fidgeting with the shortened hem of her skirt and flattening the creases of her thin blouse. Checking her back zip, she saw her weathered Bible. She closed her eyes, raising her head to face the ceiling. In a different situation I would take heed Father. For now, give me strength, she thought. Tsitsi opened her eyes and faced the mirror again. She exhaled, bringing her shoulders back, pushing her chest out and raising her chin, "Miss Malaika," she whispered, then put her hand over her mouth to suppress a giggle at the thought of herself as a beauty queen, she leaned forward again and said, "Mrs Zvobgo."

The words came dancing hurriedly from out of her mouth. They'd been turned over so many times as she tasted their deliciousness.

TSITSI GORGED herself with so much food she felt she would throw up. When she eventually returned to a semblance of normality, she called his office.

He was in a meeting, Tabitha informed her.

No, he could not be interrupted. He had given clear instructions in this regard.

No, Tabitha did not know when it would end.

Tsitsi did not trust her assurance to call only when he got out of this important, important meeting, so she continued to do so at regular intervals until Tabitha, who had now recognised the pattern, began to ignore her calls.

The next day, Tsitsi appeared at the Ministry with no appointment. The receptionist had tried to intercept her, but she proceeded regardless, pushing past him with a firm step. Tabitha was not at her desk. The door to Zvobgo's office was locked. Before she could press her ear to the door, the receptionist she had evaded had caught up to her.

"Sorry, madam, what I was trying to say is that Mr Zvobgo has gone to Headquarters. It seemed urgent—I don't know when he will be back."

Tsitsi let go of the door handle still in her grip, smiled at the man and, wordlessly, walked out of the office.

16

The two girls walked nervously to the bulletin board.

"Ini hangu, I don't think it's right that they publish our results like this. How many lives would they save if they simply posted us our results and didn't have them out here for public consumption? Those boys are already so competitive they probably slept here waiting for Professor Makumbe to put them up."

"Ah, Tsitsi, what's wrong with a little bit of competition? Those dunderheads always want to show us how smart they are, I want them to see how they've underestimated us."

"Sha, ChiChi, I'm not so sure. I finished the econometrics paper, but I left out two whole questions in the economic models section."

As they approached the board, craning their necks to see their results, one of the boys laughed as he slapped his friend on the shoulder in pre-emptive congratulations, "Blaz, vaudze! For some of us, it's not a matter of whether we passed—it's a matter of how well we passed."

Immediately, the boys began wagering on who would

have the best results, while others—the majority of students, it seemed—were already walking away sullen and unsociable. Laundry duty for the rest of the year if anyone got less than a first. $50 dollars for the best results. A swap of girlfriends if they tied.

"Hey, ladies!" Tinashe approached them and extended his hand.

"Are you asking for congratulations on your results?"

"Well, I did well, but you both did too. I'm just congratulating worthy competitors."

Tsitsi and Chiedza, feeling that he was patronising them, refused to take his hand, and pushed past him to the board to see for themselves.

"Inga zvako, Chiedza, I'm impressed! You got a distinction in statistics and passed the rest comfortably. Tsitsi, you didn't do as well in stats—just missed a distinction —but you did get one for econometrics. Who knew these two girls would be of the few who passed and did well?"

Although Tsitsi despised Takura and his friends' habit of announcing her marks before she had the opportunity to see —and absorb—them for herself, she felt the relief wash over her.

She ignored Tinashe and hugged Chiedza.

"All those prayers and nights with our feet in buckets of cold water weren't for nothing, huh?

Tsitsi laughed. "Yea, I thought you were going to kill me if I brought another one out for you."

"I would have! But it's over now—we have to celebrate. Let's go out into H-town tonight! Tonight I won't take no for an answer. Now you can't use the books as an excuse!"

Tsitsi fidgeted under Chiedza's gaze, knowing that she had no choice.

"Horaiti, horaiti—I'll come! Just let me do a few things this afternoon and then I'll join you."

"Perfect. See you in the room at six, latest. We need to get ready so we can leave by eight!"

Fretting over what she had got herself into, Tsitsi rushed to meet with the other students from the Students' Christian Organisation so they could plan their thanksgiving prayer meeting. They would hold it the following evening, the night before leaving to go home for the holidays.

The meeting had been scheduled at the beginning of the term in the faith that God would answer their prayers for academic success and there would indeed be cause for celebration for the members. A few had failed, but these exceptions were dismissed as being the cause of their own downfall.

"God helps those who help themselves," Anesu, their president, said, as he went through the roster of members in good standing, checking against another list of contributions. "Where were they when we were studying? Zvikomborero and Itai thought the answers would just appear in front of their eyes."

Tsitsi concurred, adding to the chorus of condemnation. "Futi, how do you expect to pass when you don't come to prayer meetings? You pray once and expect God to answer you? I told Itai to come, but he said he was too busy. Busy!"

Later, when Tsitsi pulled out her velvet knee-length dress, Chiedza grabbed it out of her hands as quickly as it was brought out.

"Nhai, Tsitsi, you can't wear that! Everyone will ask me why I decided to spoil the fun by bringing my little sister! We're not going to church …" She rummaged through her own cupboard and took out a short black dress. "Here, take this!"

"Chiedza, do you want me to come or don't you? Please, I'll be really uncomfortable wearing this."

Chiedza scowled and threw the dress back into her cupboard, knowing she had already won the biggest part of the battle—just getting her roommate out on the town was enough of a victory.

Nkosinathi, Chiedza's on-and-off boyfriend who worked in town, picked them up from the residence and drove them to the nightclub. He had his friend Taurai sitting in the front passenger seat, so the two settled into the backseat of the Peugeot.

Tsitsi steeled herself for an argument with Chiedza over her decision not to drink, but no sooner were they in the club, Chiedza was off with Nkosinathi, leaving her alone with Taurai.

The music blared, mostly a mix of dancehall and reggae, maintaining a jumpy rhythm that had the floor gyrating. But suddenly her line of sight was blocked and Taurai appeared in front of her. In an attempt at humour—or rather to seduce her—he began moving his hips, snaking them round and round, in that dislocated way that only a man can do. Embarrassed, she covered her face and looked away. He was persistent, though, and took her hands to his slender hips. It felt strangely erotic, enjoying the sway of a man's hips, and she tried not to look. Instead, however, she found herself hypnotised, staring at how well he mimicked the male back-up dancers in a Buju Banton music video.

As the beat of the song became more furious, so did his own movements. She was even more embarrassed, and eventually couldn't stand it any longer, and pulled her hands away, thinking of the scandal that would erupt if any member of the SCO had seen her. He smiled, satisfied, as he let her hands go. Then he leaned in and planted his lips on hers. She stood there, silent, her heart beating faster, in shock at his boldness.

He offered to buy her a drink, to which she was unable to say no.

"Cheers," he said, clinking her bottle before he took a deep gulp of his own. It was the first time she had taken a sip of alcohol that wasn't the communion wine. It was bitter and dirty-tasting, like the water from a pot of boiled chibage. Her instinct was to spit it out, but held it in her cheeks before she slowly released the liquid down her throat.

"The first sip is the hardest," he laughed as he placed his free hand on her waist, as if to encourage her to continue. Slightly embarrassed that he was aware she was a first timer, she took another, less painful sip. She couldn't say whether that was because she just wanted to get through the bottle as quickly as possible, or that the firm touch of his hand felt good as it now rubbed and kneaded her soft bum, or that it was less painful because what he had declared about difficult first sips was a scientific fact.

Again, he leaned in, and kissed her. The sensation was so pleasing and he was so persuasive that she couldn't muster the courage to tell him to stop, even as he pushed his tongue into her mouth. He only took this as encouragement by a coy lover. Soon he had his hands on her breasts, and intermittently brought up the beer bottle to her lips so that she could drink too. He grew even bolder and pushed his hands into her bra to cup her bare breasts. She tried to stop him, but he excited her, and she felt the wetness between her legs.

PANASHE CHIGUMADZI

He led her to the dance floor. He turned her around, securing her to his waist so that she felt his hardness grinding against her. She soon came alive, exhilarated, dancing herself into a sweat. He had a bottle in his hand and continued to bring it to her lips, until it was empty. They drank more, and she no longer felt shy that everyone could see as he groped her breasts and bum. They got through at least six songs before they were tired and made their way back to their spot at the bar. She stumbled to the stool, and he sat her down. She had a pounding headache and her head fell limply onto his shoulder.

He ordered another drink and gave it to her, raising his finger like a schoolteacher. "When I come back," he warned, "I want to find this bottle empty."

He disappeared in the direction of Nkosinathi and Chiedza. When he returned, he had the car keys. Tsitsi was afraid that she was only three-quarters down the bottle. To this he smiled, "I guess there will be consequences for the naughty girl who didn't finish the beer a gentleman so kindly bought for her."

She felt her head spin and she began to cry, for genuine fear of punishment. He, however, was unperturbed, and led her sternly to the car, helping her into the backseat. He lay her down on her back, as she sobbed, insisting in her stupor that she was a good girl and didn't deserve to be punished. "Don't worry," he said. "Just keep quiet and we'll sort it out."

She pleaded for him to bring another bottle so that she could finish that one and show him that she was not ungrateful.

"Shhh," he murmured, annoyed at the noise she was making, and placing a rough finger to her lips. She became increasingly delirious, shouting and crying for the bottle, resisting him as he pushed his hands up her dress. She cried, until she felt a sudden blow to her face, knocking her out.

By the time Nkosinathi and Chiedza came, banging on the windows, Taurai was in the passenger seat, sleeping. She felt the area of her left temple pounding. Her first instinct was to check if she was even clothed. She was. She then checked if she was wearing underwear. She felt the fabric now starchy dry with what had been her wetness.

There was no time to continue the inspection before Chiedza climbed into the backseat. She and Nkosinathi seemed to have had a fight. She didn't say anything to him as he drove them back to campus.

Chiedza helped Tsitsi out of the car, and said nothing when Nkosinathi shouted goodbye. Chiedza walked her no more than a couple of metres, before she stopped and helped her push her index and forefinger finger down her throat, until the alcohol in her stomach emptied into the flowerbed outside Swinton Hall. As she coughed out the last bit of spittle, she tried to get to her feet again for fear of being seen by one of the SCO members or even someone else who knew her and tell them.

She was relieved, her thoughts a little clearer, but still needed Chiedza to help her to their room. And when she finally slumped onto her bed, her head spun around mercilessly until she fell asleep, exhausted and ashamed. Impatient to forget.

17

"**G**o-go-goyi!"

Tsitsi shouted as she pushed her hand past the security gate and rapped on Chiedza's half-open door. As she drove there, she had considered turning back. She hadn't spoken to Chiedza in some time and was taking a chance she would be home. The burden of her secret had become too heavy to bear alone, and she wanted—needed—to speak to her friend. What else to do with a secret that made her sleeping pills useless?

"Ndiani?" Chiedza called out before her head appeared at the security gate. "Oh! And to what do I owe this pleasure?"

"Just thought I'd come and say hello."

"Tsitsi, don't say this as if you can just walk from Highlands! You haven't responded to any of my messages or calls—and now you are just coming to say hello?"

Tsitsi said nothing. What Chiedza said was true. But the trial didn't last, before her friend burst into a giggle, and gestured for her to come in.

"Come in, come in, tigashire! I don't know what Zvobgo

did to you, but I'm happy to have someone to watch this Nigerian movie with me. The story is so funny"

Tsitsi smiled. She loved Chiedza for her consistency.

"Why don't you give me some DVDs so I can watch at home?" Tsitsi asked, picking up a set of pirated DVDs from Chiedza's side table.

"And what happens when I want to watch the one you've taken?"

"Ah, Chiedza, you have so many! Just one."

Chiedza pretended outrage, "Just one! My sista-o! You know what I had to do to get this good ting? I was sitting all day with those boys who were pirating the movies for me! And where were you-o? Busy, busy with that Mr Zvobgo of yours! Hey!"

They laughed.

"My sista, please do sometin' about your accent."

"What are you saying-o? Abomination! They call me 'Mr Ibu's wife'! I am, as they say, the real deal! Hey!"

They settled together on Chiedza's bed to watch the movie playing on her laptop, in the same way they had when procrastinating studying for a test.

The movie was Confusion. They had chosen this over Princess Beyoncé and Blackberry Babes.

Although Tsitsi preferred love stories, and this one had more to do with witchcraft than anything else, she was nonetheless relieved that there was this distraction as they became deeply engrossed in the movie. At one point Chiedza slapped Tsitsi's arm in outrage at the turn of events in the film.

"This silly woman! Tsitsi, are you seeing this? Kunonzi kurasa pfungwa! She thinks she is Mary! She is actually praying to God for immaculate conception! In the UK those white women don't even need husbands for babies any more; they just get sperm donors and have them on their own! But maybe we shouldn't be judgemental—if she had the money she could do the same, but she doesn't, so she must now come and plead with God for silly requests! People can be so silly sometimes, nhaika?"

The woman in the movie consoled her daughter, "A woman's loyalty is tested when her man has nothing. A man's loyalty is tested when he has everything. Be strong, my child, everything will come right."

Chiedza just rolled her eyes. Tsitsi, though, was less flippant. And as the movie continued, she became more and more agitated, taking on the emotion of the characters, as if it were her own plight she faced.

"But why, Chiedza? How can Mr Ramsey do such a thing?" she asked, pained.

"Tsitsi, you need to understand. This is a disease from boyhood that men never really grow out of. The difficult thing with men is that their eyes and penises don't age."

And then, without a prelude Tsitsi finally spoke, choosing a moment when both were faced towards the screen. "Chiedza, I think you are right."

"Yes, of course I am. Ndiri kukuudza, this woman, she is going to get killed by her own son."

"No, ChiChi. I think you're right about Zvobgo."

Tsitsi was stunned by her confession, but the words had run out of her mouth now, and there was no way to get them back. She could not begin to regret telling her now. Chiedza pushed Pause and turned to face her.

"What can I do?" Silence. "Tsitsi, why are you so fixed on this idea of a white wedding? He paid roora for you, isn't that acknowledgement enough?"

"No, Chiedza." She couldn't say that it was not recognised in the eyes of the Church. "But I can't force him into a white wedding, I know. You know that a woman should never ask, or she'll push the man away."

Chiedza scrunched her face but remained quiet for a while before sitting up straight and taking Tsitsi's hand. "Tsitsi, what's the one thing you haven't given him?"

"I don't know ChiChi, what?"

"You haven't given him any children. You know people won't take any woman seriously until she's had the man's children."

"But Zvobgo already has two daughters—who are now grown women."

"Yes, but he doesn't have a son."

"Chiedza, but how could the lack of a son be a problem? He's not some rural man. He's not even very traditional. All those years he was married to Mrs Zvobgo, surely he would have left her if that was the sort of man he was? And why did they stop at two children?"

Chiedza shrugged. "Hameno, shamaz. I don't know what his reasons may have been then, but you can't rule it out, Tsitsi. You know how a man can think. Now that he is old, he might be thinking of it. Maybe that's why it was so easy for you to replace Mrs Zvobgo?"

"If he is thinking of it, he hasn't said anything."

"Have you been using protection?"

"No, we haven't ever used any."

"So maybe he thinks he can't get that from you." Chiedza didn't see the insensitivity of her comment, but Tsitsi felt the sting of the insinuation. "And you know what happens once men get an idea in their head: they become like dogs on heat. It's like they become blind—whatever has a vagina, never mind breasts or buttocks, they don't discriminate. They just want to spread their seed as far and wide as possible. At least one of these women will bear a son. Men think like that. It's so easy to become a father that it doesn't need to take an entire night, even ten minutes, five minutes, two minutes even, is enough. Zvatoita, ipapo! You'd think it would take more to do something as important as creating another life. If you want to secure him, become the mother of his children —and, if you can help it, the mother of his One and Only Son. Mira uone, Tsitsi, he'll become so attached to you."

Tsitsi wished Chiedza would stop. Just stop. And let her be.

When she didn't, Tsitsi eventually switched off. She could not bear the pressure brought on her by Chiedza's torrent of generalisations and theories on men. All it did was remind her why she had not visited Chiedza in a while.

And even if Chiedza was right to some extent, Tsitsi wasn't so sure Zvobgo would be indiscriminate. She saw him as the kind of man who had to have a singular focus, the kind where it was a zero-sum game. If he became interested in another woman for whatever reason, he would lose interest in her. One woman or another. Either/or, not and/or. The same way that he could not easily maintain her as a Small House while he was married to Mrs Zvobgo, as so many other men did. He was not the kind of man who could simultaneously maintain a legitimate family—one that would attend public functions and gatherings, and receive awards on his behalf—while keeping an illegitimate family that would only be united during the holidays while he was supposedly away on overseas trips or at the weekend under the pretext of regional and national conferences. He was either/or. She was sure of that.

With that as her conclusion, Tsitsi began to consider the implications. Perhaps what she did need to do was give him a son.

But how to guarantee that? They had not slept together in some time. And when they had, she had not become pregnant. How could she have not thought about that? Was she infertile? Was he maybe sterile? He was old, after all. Maybe that was why he could not have blamed Mrs Zvobgo for only having two daughters? Maybe, being the modern man that he was, he understood—understood that the fault lay with him.

But it didn't matter. As Chiedza often reminded her and her own mother countless times before, a man was a man. In situations like this, that biological fact stood above all else. Loyalty, reason, understanding. All that rationality would be squashed under the pressure of a growing desire for a son to continue his name.

Tsitsi's chest heaved a great sigh as Chiedza continued babbling on about her theories. She felt the familiar spinning sensation that almost had her laughing deliriously as she found herself in the same state of desperation that had seen her pursue Zvobgo. Just when she had established some semblance of stability, some sort of toehold on a decent livelihood, she felt she was now watching it slip from under her feet. It was a state that saw her mind begin to buzz with new ideas and strategies for her survival. She had not prayed for a long time, not since her failed attempt at fasting, but in her desperation, she suddenly thought of praying—prayer for the miracle of immaculate conception. She would announce to her mother that her new Christian name would be Mary. A fitting name—except, of course, that she was not a virgin but nonetheless the birth of the saviour son would have been a miracle.

She almost let out a giggle, but did not want Chiedza to see her go into her state of delirium at the ridiculousness of it all, so she stopped herself.

18

The next day she was woken by a call from Chiedza.

"Come with me to my church."

"Kupi?"

Perhaps she hadn't heard her friend right. It was not Christmas or Easter, so there was no reason for Chiedza to be going to church. Church?

"To my church."

"Chiedza, since when are you are a faithful church goer?"

"Ah, you hadn't spoken to me in a while, so you wouldn't know, would you? I'm part of the United Kingdoms of Glory Ministry. And we are firm in our faith. We just don't think that we have to turn up every Sunday, and thump the Bible at everyone we meet. And, besides, our God does not object to a drink here and there—was it not Jesus who turned water into wine?"

"Is this what these Pentecostals are telling you to lure you in?"

"Tsitsi, it's legit. I promise you. The other day I heard of a pastor in South Africa who got his congregation to believe that eating grass was the key to their salvation. That is where I draw the line. There's none of that at the United Kingdoms of Glory Ministry. It's legit."

"Ish, ChiChi, I'm not sure …"

"Look, I was given a flyer by some very good-looking members of their praise team while I was at the Book Café some weeks ago. I was also doubtful but they persuaded me to come just once, and I loved it. The music, the atmosphere, the members—I've never been to anything like it!"

Tsitsi remained silent.

"Come now, Tsitsi! Don't be like someone who can't hold two ideas in their head at the same time! Our pastor, the Prophet, understands. He lives in a world like us too. He is not some sort of ghostly saint preaching deprivation and poverty. He speaks to the God who has lived in Mbare and understands that we too want to live in Borrowdale Brook like the new money or in Highlands like the old money. It's like he really understands what it's like to be me in my situation."

"Horaiti, Chiedza, if you're so convinced, I'll come."

"Great—and don't forget your money for our contributions. It's very important, Prophet Masara believes in sowing what you want to reap from the prosperous Kingdom."

"But what if I can't contribute? Are the poor condemned to hell?"

"Aiwaka, it's not as if they are doomed to it. They need to come to United Kingdoms of Glory and invest in their faith. If you're forever begging and never giving to God and His works, how can you expect to prosper?"

So it was that they shuffled into the church with the rest of the congregation. Tsitsi's eyes scanned the place, more of an imposing air-conditioned conference centre than anything else. Her conservative sensibilities had her cringing as she eyed the congregation dressed as if it were going to be announced that today was indeed Judgement Day and appearances would be taken into account by Christ Himself. Men wore business suits, women in dresses of various lengths and varying degrees of formality—evening gowns, summer dresses and club dresses, and their children in miniature suits and gowns.

Tsitsi noticed a heavily pregnant woman wading through a crowd that had gathered in one of the corners of the large church. She wondered how this woman had got pregnant. She wasn't what she would call beautiful, the pregnancy presumably exaggerating her facial features, making them look grotesque. If she could get pregnant—that is, if she could have a man desire her and feel the urge to spread his seed inside her—then surely she, Tsitsi, could get pregnant too? This wasn't the only pregnant woman. She noticed a number of other young expectant mothers and a few who looked like they could have been past child-bearing, caressing full bellies. There seemed to be something in the water.

Once in their seats, some young girls, whose hemlines to Tsitsi's mind were too short, handed them small booklets titled The Light.

"Chi," she whispered, "this is just like The Tower."

"Mxm! Don't compare us to those heathens, Tsitsi—we are not heathens. This publication is better than that."

Prophet Masara was bent over an open ledger with dog-eared pages covered in rows of neat squares. Praise and worship! the projected PowerPoint slide behind him proclaimed.

They began the service with a medley of hymns that Tsitsi knew from her own church, only made more lively and vibrant as they were accompanied by cymbals and drums. The lyrics evoked recent developments in the country, drawing parallels with biblical events, as the congregation clapped and swayed, clapped and swayed to the music.

Some youths, all wearing the same white T-shirts bearing the words 'Praise Team' in gold cursive on the front and a big cross on the back, made their way the front of the stage and began their own urban grooves rendering of "As the deer pants for water". One began beat-boxing and another, the one with the baggiest jeans, began rapping his hook for the rendition.

And so the Prophet began, the urgency in his voice tinged with an American twang, which when Tsitsi asked why he said 'Gad' instead of 'God,' Chiedza explained it was by virtue of his having spent time in America with Pastor TD Jakes himself, which—just as impressively—had done after completing Bible Studies under TB Joshua himself.

His voice sprang out loosely, without the restraint conferred by a white collar. Instead, he wore a silver tie to match his silver suit. He marched through the mass of his acolytes and choristers. Then came the sermon. He started slowly, calmly, as if in a whisper, only gradually raising his tone. Then came the dramatic changes in voice and gesture, as he sang, cajoled, pleaded, condemned and promised.

"Why? Why, Lord?" he screamed out in anguish, suddenly tearing his shirt—under which, fortunately, he wore another —and began beating his chest, acting out his humiliation. "Why do you forsake me? Why, Gad, why?" He chanted, stumbling across the stage, and then collapsing into a chair. He now looked as if he was weeping. Tsitsi felt embarrassed watching a grown man cry and found herself scanning the rest of the congregation in search of similar sentiment.

"Oh, Gad! Oh, my Gad, my Gad of Abraham and Isaac," he implored plaintively, "we need You, we need You, we need YOU! Almighty!"

He was standing now, his voice reaching fever pitch, arousing the congregation who were now grunting and groaning in agreement, encouraging him further.

"We need You to do for us what You did for Your children of Israel! Father, we too, Your children, need You to free us! Free us from oppression! Free us from these chains of slavery! Free us, Lord! Free us, Gad! Free us!"

He began to pace, back and forth, back and forth, restlessly across the stage as he further implored the Lord, gaining clarity in his wishes for his congregation.

"Free us! Lord, free us! Free us so that you can lead us! Lead us! Lead us! Lead us through these hot deserts burning our souls, Gad! Lead us through the roaring seas drowning our spirits, Gad! Lead us, Lord! Lead us and scatter our enemies! Take us through this Exodus! Take us through these trials and tribulations! As You did for us all those millenniums ago! Lead us as You did Abraham and Isaac!"

Millennia, Tsitsi wanted to correct him, but she had to admit that when he spoke, he did so with the conviction of someone who had actually witnessed the Exodus himself. Tsitsi saw that many of the congregation were now standing, many with hands in the air, palms facing upwards to receive the Lord's spirit. Not wanting to identify herself as a non-believer, she too stood and mimicked the rest, raising her hands heavenward.

Then, suddenly, he stopped. The lights on the stage dimmed such that there was only one spotlight, and it shone down on the Prophet himself, as if he were the Anointed One. The crowd fell silent too.

He began now in a furious whisper, "And now, you followers, listen as I say, you must turn to me! Turn away from all of your worldly belongings and surrender! Surrender your house! Your car! Your husband! Your wife! Your Small House! Leave them all for me and you will receive glorious prosperity in my Golden Kingdom! For I have said, he who is first shall be last! And ...?"

He pointed the microphone at his congregation of acolytes, motioning that they should complete his commandment.

"He who is last shall be first!"

The Prophet was now assuming the voice of God Himself, which terribly offended Tsitsi's sensibilities, and yet it catapulted the rest of the church into a celebratory uproar with the excitement of schoolchildren who had answered their teacher correctly.

"I can't hear you! My followers, speak to me! He ...?"

It was all proving too much for Tsitsi. His performance was, in her mind, strained. She had no desire for this kind of visceral experience of God.

"He who is last shall be first!"

"He ...?"

"He who is last shall be first!"

Now the cymbals and drums started up again, turning this call-and-response into a lively chorus. The Prophet was now jumping about on the stage.

"He ...?"

"He who is last shall be first!"

The chorus continued with liberal improvisations. And, as they did, an assistant brought the Prophet a towel for he was sweating heavily now. Another brought him a bottle of water branded with the church logo. Once the Prophet had finished the water, he positioned himself at the centre of the stage once again.

He dabbed at the beads of sweat gathering once more on his brow. He took a deep breath and his biblical speak gave way to the more pressing needs of modernity. "Lord! The complexities and the possibilities and the flexibilities! Lord, they are ours! They are ours! Because we are the chosen children! The children of a King! We are princes and princesses in His Holy Kingdom! His heirs, the heirs to the prosperous Kingdom of God! Yes, the prosperity of the Kingdom is ours! Can you believe it?"

Tsitsi found she was the only one jarred by the sudden shift in the sermon's direction. The church boomed in response!

"Yes! Indeed we are the heirs to the glorious, prosperous Kingdom of God! Yes! Don't be fooled by those who say your destiny is to be poor! Let me tell you, so that you can tell them! Your destiny is to be prosperous! You are to be prosperous, not paupers, as they tell you. Because we, my brothers and sisters, are princes and princesses of the King of Kings!"

The congregation leapt about in affirmation.

"Yes! Yes! So, you princes and princesses, speak! Speak unto Him and tell Him, your Father, the King of all Kings! Tell Him all of your desires! For the Lord, the King of Kings, has told us to ask! Ask, my people! Ask and you shall receive!"

He had slipped back into biblical language and the room burst into a further cacophony, becoming the Tower of Babel before Tsitsi's eyes and ears. Tsitsi tried to close her eyes in prayer and, like all around her, implore the Lord for His mercy, but she could hardly hear her own thoughts. She was particularly distracted by the woman next to her who was praying feverishly in words that appeared little more than a babble. The woman, hands raised, was hyperventilating and she soon began weeping, sobbing, but continued through her ragged breaths, praying, chanting in sentences without structure or form and words that had lost meaning. Speaking in tongues. Tsitsi saw too, out of the corner of her eye, that Chiedza was muttering just as hard, albeit quietly to herself.

"And those who want blessings, those who want the prosperity, come to the fore that we may bless you! Come, come, my children. Come!"

People began to make their way to the front of the stage where a number of the assistant preachers had gathered. Tsitsi watched as Chiedza joined them. The assistants had their palms squarely on the foreheads of those congregants determined to share in the Lord's gifts, the Lord's prosperity.

Even though the Prophet was in the service of God, she found it difficult to take in as congregants gathered around him, eyes shut and palms reaching heavenward, imploring God, pleading for their desires. Speedy approval of visas. Exams passed with eight, even, ten points. Travel mercies for those on their way to buy wares in Johannesburg and Gaborone. Success for borehole businesses.

"If you don't receive, it is because your faith is not strong enough. You need to believe!" the Prophet commanded as if prompted by Tsitsi's disbelief.

The woman next to her shrieked and suddenly she was on the floor, tremors wracking her body. Alarmed, Tsitsi just stood, still. Those around her continued in their worship, some looking on at the woman with what appeared to be envy. Another, overcome by feverish trembling, fell to her knees and began intoning in prayer. The entire congregation was now in fits of joyous hysteria. Some were falling about, some weeping. Some both.

Tsitsi quickly picked up her bag and pushed through the congregation to get outside to her car. This was now too much for her.

He who is first shall be last. He who is last shall be first. He who is first shall be last. He who is last shall be first. She heard the words of the Prophet like a looping song in her mind.

If she were honest, she had always been suspicious of purported Men of God who had no disdain for wealth. Was it that she enjoyed Fata Marwira begging for donations every week? Maybe she did. Though she didn't aspire to the same sort of life for herself, it offered her a sense of superiority in this world that she wasn't guaranteed in the afterlife. Suffering, deprivation, hardship were all important aspects of discipleship, of communion with Jesus Christ, who had spent forty days in the wilderness, tempted and taunted by Satan. This prosperity gospel was not for her.

Chiedza suddenly appeared at the door of the car, pulled it open and climbed in.

"Tsitsi, don't be so holier than thou! You're just like every other Christian who believes that their interpretation of the Bible is the right one, that everyone else is misguided." Tsitsi saw the fire in Chiedza's eyes. "The other day I heard a group of women from my mom's church say they asked God through their Pastor to take their desire for sex away —and the Pastor obliged! I don't get it, but that's how it is."

Tsitsi didn't answer her.

"I like to see the act of faith in Christianity as mixing

Mazoe. It's a 'dilute-to-taste' thing, but at the end of the day, we are all drinking Mazoe." Still no response from Tsitsi. "Anyway, I'm going back in now. The praise team is having a meeting after the sermon and I want to join them."

Still riding the wave of elevation conjured up in the church, Chiedza left the matter there.

19

The relatives, especially those from Baba's side, were hysterical, too present, too eager to help and demonstrate their grief. Mama remained stoic and dignified as they took charge over the proceedings and took stock of his belongings.

At the graveside she listened to speeches that extolled the virtues that, although she loved her father, she never knew he had. But that didn't matter then because now he had passed into the world of the venerable.

She was already tired by the time the day had begun. The night before, Tsitsi and her mother had managed to steal away and hold a private vigil for themselves. The sleeping bodies of relatives lay everywhere, so they chose the kitchen, where Baba's closed coffin lay. Seeing Tsitsi's hesitance at crossing the threshold into the room, Mama took her by the hand and brought her in. Tsitsi felt the warmth of her embrace as they sat on the reed mat they used when they cooked on the fire together. The timbre of Mama's voice as she began a soft whisper of the Lord's Prayer comforted her and had her more at ease in the presence of her father's dead body. She joined Mama in her intonation. They continued to pray in unison, gently rocking together, until the new day broke. They didn't go back inside until they had boiled pots of water with which the more important visitors could wash.

Now, the longer she stood at the graveside, she heard less and less of what anyone was saying about Baba; instead, she felt a sense of her consciousness freeing itself from her body. Her fatigue was made worse by the dizzying heat of the funeral day. She had seen that the clouds bore the portents of rain and soon there was a welcome drizzle. She watched at the graveside as the priest, Fata Masika, murmured prayers over her father's coffin.

As the pain of the day clawed deeper and deeper in her heart, she felt her legs grow longer and longer, until she, giraffe-like, stood tall, looking over the head of Babamukuru Edzai, the tallest man there. She had the sense of her childish thoughts and preoccupations being the catalyst of the woman she had become, and she resolved to become her mother's protector.

As the pain subsided, she returned to her body, her senses sharpened. She looked down at her mother at her side and, noticing the teardrops, reached over to gently wipe them away. She felt her mother's body in silent tremble, one that seemed to have intensified as the proceedings went on. She embraced her then, arresting the despairing tremor of her spirit. She held her until the ceremony ended and people began filtering from the burial ground and made their way to the homestead. The funeral-goers moved in a slow snake of a procession that slowly began to disintegrate as they eased themselves out of solemnity and stopped to enquire about one another's health and the weather and the crops where they came from.

When the last person was out of sight, Tsitsi exhaled heavily in a way that seemed to release the troubled air inside of her.

"Mama, I'm here. Please don't cry."

"I'm not crying, mwanangu."

Sensing that her reassurance had done nothing to resolve her daughter's anguish, she held her tighter and continued in a sombre voice, "Women can't cry when they must get on."

She wanted to ask her mother whether men could cry then, but the older woman was already walking, making her way to the house, getting on.

As she stood there watching the figure of her retreating mother, head down, shoulders hunched, she felt a sudden urgency, an impatience to return to boarding school. This—school—could change their lot in life. She imagined an older version of herself driving Mama to town in her own car, perhaps to the shops to buy whatever she chose, not according to need but to choice and preference and then taking her back to the house she had bought for her in Harare where she would be free of all backbreaking work because she would have electricity, which she could use liberally, and a house girl to do what couldn't be done by machine. Tsitsi's heart raced as she thought of this. She felt a veneer of seriousness, a determination glaze over her, hardening into a newly acquired virtue.

That afternoon, people gathered in the living room and outside the canopy, the older women and men on chairs pushed up against the wall, the younger women who weren't part of the cooking duty on the floor, all praying out loud.

The younger men lingered outside talking about nothing but
the cars they had seen on their journey there.

She hardly recognised their homestead. With the throng
of relatives, it had lost its familiarity and turned into an
uncertain place. She didn't know where to sit. She was
attended to by her aunts, her father's sisters, in a cold
manner that seemed to be in correspondence with their
brothers.

As the day dragged on an ugliness began to rear its head,
rapidly displacing the pretences of sympathy. She wanted to
go with Mama when her uncles took her to the n'anga, but
she was held back. Mama had resisted fiercely. Mama herself
had never mixed traditional beliefs and her Christianity.
There was no room for any sort of duality; the adoption of
one meant the wholesale rejection of the other. And, sure
enough, her daughter had been inculcated in this. Her uncles
knew this. Where she was usually quiet and tolerant, in this
the older woman had always been militant and never
hesitated to show her disdain.

When Tsitsi's father was still alive, and the tsikamutanda
had made an unsolicited visit to their village with the
mission of helping its denizens identify the troublesome
witches in their midst, Mama had summarily dismissed him
as a charlatan and barred him from crossing the threshold
into their homestead. She had gone even further and
denounced him and his work in front of the church,
imploring them to banish this heathen. She had even fought
her husband, and refused to accommodate him in any way.
They had seen all of this.

When she had had trouble conceiving and was advised to
go and see the n'anga, she had refused, saying she believed in
the promise of her God. If her husband was to leave her, then

it must be God's will. They had seen this too. When she had been sick, she was unwavering in her commitment to attending mass. Even this they had seen. And yet that did not stop them from harassing her today, the day she had buried her husband, until she eventually gave in and went with them to the n'anga. Tsitsi wondered if this was just a means for dissuading Mama of any claims to their brother's property or a genuine witchhunt by his bereaved family who perhaps thought her public rejection of their traditions was a decoy for her true beliefs. Perhaps they believed that there was no natural way that their brother could have met his terrible fate of being in the line of a drunken driver.

The allegations of witchcraft on the part of her mother had begun when, years after Tsitsi's birth and no son, or child for that matter, to speak of, her father had not given in to his brother's demands that he take another wife or leave Tsitsi's mother. Mama had stood her ground when he had relayed their message to her. She had said calmly, "If you take another one, so be it. I will not be here. Leave if you must."

It was not that Baba was not concerned for this lack of a son. He thought that, as long as they continued trying, their time would come. It had, after all, been after a long time and with some struggle that they had had Tsitsi. In the few years after Tsitsi's birth, they had suffered three miscarriages until she had put her foot down and decided that no further pregnancies would ensue.

For this, the uncles had called her a witch. What kind of mupfuhwira had she got that he couldn't leave her? She wasn't even beautiful, they had said at a meeting where they confronted their brother for the umpteenth time. They had ambushed him, arriving at his household when both Tsitsi and her mother were there. They spoke freely, not bothered that Mama would hear. That she heard them would not have been unusual anyway because they said it often enough to her face.

As Tsitsi sat alone outside the granary, she remembered her uncles' confrontational ways. Her child's mind imagined what terrible things they must be doing to her mother in that place, at the n'anga, surrounded by their vindictiveness. What if she died in there?

As she waited for Mama's return, Tsitsi felt her heart beat hard in frustration at her inability to help. She made a wager with God. If He were to help her and ensure nothing happened to her mother, she would do all she could to glorify Him.

For the rest of the time that she waited, she found herself taking refuge in her mother's copy of the Old Testament, reading and rereading verses that her mother had underlined, as a means of directly connecting with the source of strength from which her mother so often drew.

When she returned the next day, Tsitsi's uncles smugly satisfied with themselves, Mama maintained her stoic dignity. She did not say anything of it, only instructing Tsitsi to pack up her most important belongings as they would be leaving to go and stay with Sekuru Dickson in Harare for a while. As they walked to the bus stop, Tsitsi wondered if it was perhaps God's grace that her family had not chased them out and that they were able to leave with their heads held high, dignified.

TWELVE MONTHS AFTER HIS DEATH, it took a week for all their relatives to fill her father's homestead. On the Friday there was a subdued excitement as a bull was driven to the centre of the danga that Baba had built and ceremonially presented to the family, the aunts, uncles, nephews, brothers and neighbours too. The bull was sprinkled with traditional beer brewed specially by Mai Mabika, chosen because she was long past menstruation.

Tsitsi watched Mama who walked unblinking as she accompanied Babamukuru Edzai, Baba's eldest brother, who carried the hari frothing with Mai Mabika's beer. Tsitsi thought he looked especially proud of this opportunity to assert his authority as head of the family. Mama walked as if she was sleepwalking, looking straight ahead of her, dignified but all the same defiant, as the revellers followed them to Baba's grave in dense silence.

Sekuru Dickson had persuaded Mama to go back with Tsitsi for the ceremony. After all, they were family. They had paid roora. It was only right pachivanhu.

Babamukuru Edzai knelt at the graveside, and placed the beer alongside his brother's grave. Dirtying his smart grey pants, he expertly inspected the ground to ensure that there had been no tampering with the leaves or soil. He then gave a grunt of satisfaction, causing the women to break into their ululations and the men to begin the cascade of clapping cupped hands. A slow realisation of expectation pulled them down into a pregnant silence, making way for Babamukuru to relieve them again with his next words.

"My brother, it is me, and as you can see, I am accompanied by all, all of them, your blood."

At this point Mama suddenly turned on her heels and walked furiously in the direction of the homestead once belonging to Baba and her but that Babamukuru had now taken as his own. This would be the final humiliation at the hands of his family. Tsitsi knew to follow.

This disturbed the proceedings as some called after their late brother's wife. The witch who had killed him.

Mama didn't answer.

20

"Tsitsi, I'm pregnant," Chiedza said without any preamble.

She had to repeat herself because Tsitsi stood unresponsive without any gestures to indicate that she had heard. She was confused. Chiedza had been drinking and smoking, as always. She scanned her body for signs that she was showing—plump cheeks, a curved back, bump in her belly. Nothing! If anything, she had lost weight.

"ChiChi, how far along are you?"

"Fifteen weeks ... I don't know how I didn't see it for so long." She sucked her lips in irritation.

"Have you told, err ..." Tsitsi paused, thinking who she might name as the father. "Have you told the father?"

"Yes, I've told John—told him the bad news." Chiedza's American lover, Tsitsi remembered he had been getting serious.

"But, ChiChi, this is a blessing from God. Is he willing to marry you? I thought he was getting serious about you."

"Marry him? Tsitsi, I don't love him enough for that. I'm

not going to love that man out of sympathy or gratitude. He suggested it, yes, but I said no."

"But I thought we agreed that love isn't necessary for a marriage? We agreed that it's a decision about what makes the most sense. Surely you don't want the children to be accused of being bastards?"

"No, there will be no bastards or legitimate children. I'm not having it. Which is why I called you—I need you to take me to the clinic. Will you? I really don't want to go by myself."

Tsitsi felt the words pummel her stomach. She felt anger in her belly, anger at God who had betrayed her by blessing an ungrateful womb instead of her own willing one. She pushed against her belly, as if against the anger she felt, and opened her eyes.

"Chiedza, you're so far along and this is the third time now—what if you can't have children when you eventually do want them?"

"I'll cross that bridge when I get there. Right now I don't want this one. I can't."

Tsitsi remained quiet, unconsciously caressing her own belly. Maybe this was God's plan? What if ChiChi gave the baby to me? A tear rolled down her cheek as she saw her own desperation. What? Are you going to fake a pregnancy? Tsitsi, don't be silly now, she reprimanded herself. Even if she wanted to, everyone would be whispering that Zvobgo's girlfriend had cheated on him with a white man and here was the coloured baby to prove it. And, colour aside, Zvobgo himself would know this miracle baby was not his; she could count the number of times they had been intimate in the last few months. Tsitsi breathed a pained sigh.

"Will you take me?"

"Chiedza, even at those clinics, the nurses won't agree to such a late pregnancy."

"With the normal fee they won't."

"Chiedza, that's dangerous. It's also wrong. This is God's child."

Chiedza looked hurt, "I didn't call you for judgement. I called you for support—a friend's support. How many times have I been there for you?"

Tsitsi felt her stomach cramp. She was disappointed in herself, disappointed that she found it so difficult to help her friend who had indeed helped her in so many instances of uncertainty.

NOT CONSIDERING that people might gossip that Zvobgo's girlfriend was seen outside the private house in Glen Lorne known as an abortion clinic, Tsitsi parked her Land Cruiser right in front of it. She didn't think of this as she thought about her own desire for a child.

Just imagine, the situation highlighted in an H-Metro headline: 'SMALL HOUSE CAUGHT AT SLAUGHTER HOUSE!' But she was too consumed by her own thoughts to consider this.

She was struck by the number of people in the waiting room, many of them young, beautiful girls. Many of them there with whom she assumed were boyfriends. Some of them white. She was also struck by the cleanliness of the place, which was reinforced by the pungent smell of ammonia. She felt consoled by this. She remembered her mother imploring her that "Cleanliness is next to Godliness" and felt the irony bite at her heart.

Chiedza filled out her forms expertly. The illegality of the place did not translate into a lack of professionalism, which comforted Tsitsi so much that she almost forgot the circumstances for her visit to the place.

They struggled to find seats adjacent to each other, but eventually found two at the back of the room. They were quiet as they held hands. It wasn't long before a nurse called for Chiedza.

Tsitsi gave her hand a squeeze, but stayed seated as Chiedza followed the nurse, eyes front and without turning back. Tsitsi stayed behind, and decided to distract herself by retrieving a copy of TRUELOVE magazine from a glass table in the waiting room. She guessed the owner of the place must have picked it up while in South Africa and, having made so much money from the establishment, it seemed as though there must have been regular trips.

On the cover ...

TRUELOVE

30 Life with the Queen Bee: Time out with Generations' Sophie Ndaba

35 Handling the In-Laws

38 Seven Signs Your Man Is Cheating

41 Best Positions for Baby-Making Weather

66 Mxit, Facebook & Diaries: When it's okay to spy on your child

132 From Drakensberg to Delmas: Ten best local winter holidays

140 Décor Diva: At home with Basetsana Kumalo

. . .

Inside the magazine ...

FEATURES

FASHION AND BEAUTY

REGULARS

FOOD
113 Sis Dora's Kitchen

WIN! COMPETITIONS AND SPECIAL OFFERS
85 Subscription offer

HER HEART LEAPT a little before she flicked to page 38.

She felt ashamed that this was what was occupying her attention while her dear friend was having her insides scraped and diced up by an indifferent nurse.

IN HER WEAKENED STATE, Chiedza slept throughout the drive back to her flat. Barely able to walk, Tsitsi had to help her up the stairs.

Tsitsi boiled a pot of water on the stove before she helped Chiedza undress and get into the bathtub. Despite the heat, Chiedza shivered at the touch of the wet facecloth on her back. She sat hunched on her heels, trembling feverishly. Tsitsi put the cloth down and, just as she had held her mother all those years ago at her father's graveside, she pulled her close in an attempt to arrest her shaking.

They remained in this position, both weeping tearlessly, as the light began to fade.

21

"**M**ar—"
She stopped herself after the first syllable, thinking it better not to alert the rest of the house staff that she was summoning Mary. She didn't want to give them any further ammunition—they were already looking for ways to undermine her.

So she got up instead and went in search of the girl. She found her in the scullery, softly singing her melancholic hymn, with a high and plaintive voice, as she washed dishes. For a moment Tsitsi listened, thinking how she sounded like an angel. But she was quickly brought back to earth from her heavenly thoughts by the clinking and clattering of the crockery Mary washed so absent-mindedly. Softly she slapped the girl on the arm in a gesture so silly that she became even more irritated at herself. Mary jumped and nearly dropped the plate she was rinsing.

"Mary! How many times must I tell you not to throw the china in the water like that! Really, if you keep doing this I will make you pay for it!"

Poor Mary began apologising profusely. Tsitsi immediately softened her demeanour.

"I was looking for you. Once you finish what you are doing, please come up to my bedroom," she said before turning and leaving a confused Mary behind in the kitchen.

It wasn't long before she heard a faint knock on the door.

"Come in!" Another gentle knock. "Come in!"

Impatiently, she got up and pulled the door open to a shrinking Mary. When she crossed the threshold into the room she had been forbidden from entering, looking so timid, she looked like her greatest wish in the world was to disappear. Again Tsitsi felt guilty for the way in which she had so acutely evoked the image of the capricious white madams for whom Mama had worked so tirelessly during school holidays.

As she looked at Mary, Tsitsi was reminded of the convention that dictated that even when one can afford many house girls, one must never allow them to cook for your husband. Instead, you, as the Wife, the Woman of the House, must ensure that you prepare his food and serve him yourself. In addition, one must never allow another woman to wash his underwear. This applied to every woman, no matter what position she held in life. Housewife to a pauper. Housewife to a king. Whether you were a banker, businesswoman, beautician, no matter—this principle needed to be applied. Otherwise, you were quite simply leaving the door wide open for a house girl to usurp you and take your place as the Woman of the House.

Tsitsi felt a sudden shot of paranoia. She tried to reassure herself that it had been Zvobgo himself who had insisted that she never cook. That no wife of his would have to do anything around the house.

Mary stood waiting at the foot of the bed. She was older than Tsitsi by a few years but, drowning in her faded overalls, she looked like a young girl. As Tsitsi lingered, she thought how beauty had mischievously landed on this unassuming rural girl. Even with her severely cut virgin hair she was attractive. Physical perfection effortlessly manifested itself in her. Tsitsi was unnerved. The realisation that in front of her stood a potential threat pushed all reservations about what she was about to ask out of her mind.

"Where can I find a suitable n'anga? A woman specifically?" she asked in English, in order to maintain the social distance she so actively worked to cultivate in the house.

Mary remained muted by her disbelief at the question, until she finally asked, "Excuse me, madam?"

"Are you deaf?" Tsitsi hissed, annoyed at both Mary's ignorance and innocent beauty. "I want to know where I can find an n'anga, one who is female. Do you know one or don't you?"

Mary was reluctant, but seeing Tsitsi's impatience, she spoke: "Mai Matumbu. 8 Chiremba Road, Zengeza 4, Chitungwiza. That is where Gladys from next door went when she was having problems with her husband. She caught him with another woman."

"I am not having problems in my marriage," Tsitsi snapped. Mary averted her eyes and fixed them on the woven details of the Persian rug under her feet. Tsitsi went on, "So … Is he, Gladys's husband … Did he ever do it again?"

"N-n-no. She hasn't found any other woman," Mary said softly, her eyes remaining on the floor.

"Good. So, do you have her number for me?"

"I don't have it any more, but I can get it for you."

"Good. Write it on a piece of paper, but don't write anything else except that number. I don't want to see any names."

"Of course, madam, I will do that."

"Thank you, Mary. You can go now."

But before Mary could get out of the bedroom, Tsitsi grabbed her arm. "If you tell anybody about this …"—she paused and tightened her grip as she now spoke in Shona—"If you tell Baba Zvobgo, vakangonzwa chete kuti takambotaura—I will make sure you go back to your mother's village. Do you hear me?"

"E-e-he, Mama," Mary said, sounding as if she wanted to cry. "Ndazvinzwa."

"Good." Tsitsi let go of the girl's arm and sat back down on the bed, somewhat unsettled by the person she had become.

22

Long before she had ever thought to visit an n'anga, it was Zvobgo who had first introduced her to the world of the ancestors and spirits.

At the height of internal dissension, he had had an apoplectic reaction to his informants' speculation on an attempted coup. That was when he fired his old security contingent and hired the Congolese. He had told her that he would have them driven to a village in Bvumba, near the Mozambican border, to the compound of a svikiro. One with a most trusted reputation as a powerful communicator with the ancestors. Zvobgo wished to communicate his need for protection to his mudzimu. Tsitsi had protested. She would not be a part of it, she had said. Over her dead body. If he must, then he had better go alone.

She had pushed up from the bed, but had been caught by his firm, rigid grip.

"Let me not repeat myself. You are coming."

Her skin pinched between his fingers and she had felt the

bloodlessness of her forearm. She was overcome by the resoluteness in his voice and became limp in his grip.

THE SPIRIT MEDIUM, the acolyte nechombo, Zvobgo and Tsitsi were alone in his dark, smoke-filled hut. The ngoma, a flute and mbira provided a repetitive, persistent and hypnotic beat, unceasing throughout the vigil. The beat vibrated throughout her body, conjuring a heightened sense of panic within her as Zvobgo knelt in front of the svikiro.

How could he, Zvobgo, be so comfortable in the presence of the svikiro? He was hideous, almost as if that would add to the veracity of his abilities. Immortality seemed to pervade the dark, unwrinkled leathery skin of this tall, silver-maned man. Tsitsi had never seen Zvobgo subordinate himself before anyone. But here he held the svikiro as one superior, powerful and authoritative.

The svikiro ascended into hysteria, his breath accelerating into what seemed to be hyperventilation as the drumbeat became louder and increasingly rigorous. He then slipped into a full trancelike state, grunting and roaring like a lion, then whistling like a bird, as he became host to the spirit.

Zvobgo went further down onto his knees, dirtying his tailored pants, and began clapping and ululating out of respect for the mudzimu who was about to communicate to him through the svikiro. The hoarse, guttural mutterings of the mudzimu were only sometimes coherent; at other times he spoke in what Tsitsi could only describe as tongues. Zvobgo hung on to the words of the nechombo, who communicated with the svikiro, putting to him Zvobgo's questions and in turn translating his responses for Zvobgo's benefit.

Tsitsi's heart beat faster when the svikiro approached her. She flinched when he placed his hand on her. His voice rose but she heard no words. She was clamouring for breath as her heart now hammered in her chest. Tears filling her eyes, she bit her lower lip hard until she punctured it, causing it to bleed. She squeezed her eyes shut as she tried to decide— 'Hail Mary' or 'Our Father?'

"Our Father, who art in heaven," she began breathlessly. What had she got herself into? Her thoughts became as frenzied as the drum beat. "Hallowed be Thy name. Thy Kingdom come. Thy will be done on Earth as it is in Heaven." —Eternal perdition, she thought. She saw the gnashing of teeth and tall flames burning. "Give us this day our daily bread." —Have I have sold my soul to the devil? "Forgive us our debts, as we forgive our debtors." —But I did not come of my own free will. "And lead us not into temptation, but deliver us from evil." —If I'm going to die now, Lord, for this venial sin ... Father, it is inadvertent. For that, mea maxima culpa. "For Thine is the Kingdom ..." She was so absorbed that she did not notice that the svikiro had left her and the beat had stopped. "The power and the glory, forever and ever. Amen."

She shut her eyes, closed them tight, and waited for the worst. Maybe she was a different kind of believer? Perhaps her faith could survive this? It had not been her doing, after all. She shivered. She struggled to regulate her breathing. Her diaphragm contracting and expanding exaggeratedly, her rib cage felt as if it would give in, that it would burst as her breast lurched so hard. She felt light headed as the voices and sounds around her became distant and eventually inaudible.

As THEY DROVE BACK she found herself in what could only be described as a stupor, her body in shock.

Seated in the back of his Prado with Zvobgo, she shut her eyes tight, pretending to sleep, but really shutting down any opportunity to speak. She wanted to be alone with her thoughts. She chided herself for being so melodramatic. It was not unheard of for people to do these things, so why should she feel like this? As if she had been violated. As if she had crossed some unspeakable Rubicon. People pick and choose, with the same ease and fluidity of going kumusika and choosing different items from the vendors.

They picked without discrimination, simply according to the most attractive offering at the time. Why was it so difficult for Tsitsi? What made her so special? Perhaps it was also because she had not expected it from Zvobgo?

That night she could not sleep. She was helpless and pathetic in her thoughts. Throughout her life, in moments of crisis she had been buoyed by her intercession with God. Now she pulled the blanket over her head like a child afraid of the dark, using the blanket as protection against whatever evil lurked in the inky-black mass that surrounded her.

She closed her eyes, and began to search for words to implore her God for forgiveness. She wanted the words to speak of her repentance. But how could she when she was now so deeply involved? She had not gone of her own volition. Zvobgo, who was sleeping more restfully now than she had seen in months, had strong-armed her into doing it. But had she not made the original wager with this sin when she had sought Zvobgo out? Even so, she could not have forseen this. This was too far.

She tried busying herself by tracing the shadowy outlines of the furniture in the room, attempting to push out all thoughts from her mind. If she could simply still her thoughts, then it wouldn't be so difficult.

Eventually, exhausted from the back and forth in her mind, she finally settled on the fact that it was not of her own choice. None of it was. She had been forced by circumstance to approach Zvobgo. Equally, she had been forced by Zvobgo to visit the svikiro. That was that. She had had no real say in any of it. She was simply a passive player in a game with fate that had long been set up and determined without any regard for her own wishes.

She wondered if this was the first time he had done this. She doubted as much—he looked far too comfortable. She then wondered if Mrs Zvobgo had ever been subjected to forays such as these. Her mind began to race again.

Perhaps she should have been grateful that he wanted her to come with him? That he had taken her into his confidence and insisted that she be part of this ritual that was so important to him. Perhaps this meant her place in the household, in the Main House, was secured. He had crossed a Rubicon with her. Surely that bound them together in ways that a simple marriage certificate could not? If he could expose her to such, she was surely more than just a body? Perhaps a pillar of support for him, then?

She laughed quietly to herself, that this might have been the price of security. That this was the sign she had been looking for. This was what her life had come to. How different was it really from selling her soul to the devil?

While she wrestled with her thoughts, Zvobgo had long fallen into a small death beside her, his body loose, without any tension. This, as she lay ramrod straight on her side of the bed.

The visit to the svikiro went undiscussed. Tsitsi remained haunted by the ordeal and lay awake for nights until she started taking sleeping pills. She could no longer pray. Zvobgo, on other hand, seemed to have a renewed sense of authority and power. He seemed invigorated against his plotters, as if he were invincible. Or at least he was reassured that the enmity had been eliminated or greatly reduced.

The sense of unreality persisted well into the remainder of the year until she successfully forced the memory into the dark annals of her mind.

23

Tsitsi rushes out of the n'anga's room to her Land Cruiser to escape the cold air and the pungent smell of smoke from burning piles of refuse. She holds her nose like someone who has never lived in the township.

She looks down to see that soot from the floor has sullied the bottom of her skirt. She wears dark shades to cover her sleep-deprived eyes.

The flailing arms of a policewoman bring Tsitsi out of her distracted gaze as they flag her down. She stops just in front of the spikes laid out across the road as the officer approaches the window of the vehicle.

As Tsitsi opens the tinted window she is able to see clearly both the policewoman and a young policeman behind her, leaning against a drum, looking decidedly unauthoritative and uninterested in his duties.

"Makadii, Mama?"

"Takasimba," she says without turning to face her.

"Tokumbira driver's licence kana ID."

They should know who she is. Why should they need to ask for identification?

"Sisi, you know who I am. Why are you stopping me?"

Her colleague approaches the car. "Mama, we are only doing our job. Strict orders from the top."

Still Tsitsi does not turn, but reaches for her licence in the side pocket of her handbag. "Suit yourselves."

Turning to face the policeman, she sees his eyes in the shadow of his navy-blue cap. He has adopted a familiarity with her that makes him comfortable enough to stare openly. Who is he? His eyes penetrate hers and she soon recognises them. Takura Kanyangarara, her former classmate. Before she can escape the eye contact, he recognises her.

"Tsitsi? Ndiwe? Is this really you in this car? Vagoni, Shef! Life must be treating you well!"

Realising that any attempt at ignoring him any further will be futile, she responds, "Yes Takura, it's me." She says this in English, with an outstretched hand holding her licence out to him. "It's up to date. No expiry."

Although taken aback, he keeps the eye contact, boring further into her eyes. He doesn't blink as a smile grows on his face. He takes the licence to reconfirm that it is indeed Tsitsi. He narrows his eyes at the photograph and lifts it up to the last rays of the setting sun, to the same level as her face, contemplating the contrast between the thumbnail black-and-white crop-haired face and the life-size full-colour head-wrapped face. The woman in front of him is not the meek girl he knew to always accept the jibes he threw at her.

His eyebrows rise into an arc as he continues to stare, unblinking, while her eyes search the floor of the Land Cruiser, careful to avoid his. Her left hand fumbles in her handbag over lipstick, mascara and cards for notes. Before she can lift the notes out of her bag, he stops her.

"That won't be necessary. We are doing our job, keeping the roads safe in this time of election hooliganism."

Hooliganism. She smiles, thinking of how gritting his showcases of vocabulary had been when they were in class together. He hands her the licence and returns to slump on the drum, his duty discharged.

As Tsitsi drives away, the rosary Mama had once draped over the rear-view mirror for "safety and protection" seems to mock her for dabbling in mashopeshope. No, I will not to be chastised by a rosary, she thinks. In a different situation, yes. In this one, no.

It was not her fault. Zvobgo compelled her to do it. She has a university degree and yet he and all of her prospective employers offered her peanuts for a tedious administrative post. What was she to do with the peanuts that barely stretched as far as the kombi fare to and from work? Peanuts that have even brought her to contemplate becoming a border-jumper like a caged monkey?

No, I will not to be chastised by a rosary, she thinks. In a different situation, yes, but in this one, no. How else can she be with a man like Zvobgo?

Tsitsi slips her hand into her bag and closes sweaty fingers around the bottle. She begins to feel tense. She closes her eyes. This is necessary.

She steels herself and, once out of the car, her steps are light and quick. She keeps her head down, eager to avoid eye contact with the security guards and with the office staff there.

Is this, this consulting with the n'anga, a mortal or venial sin? she asks herself as she gathers strength to enter the reception. Whatever it is, does it count considering my leave of absence from church? No, this cannot be classified as that. This is temporary until such time that she is ready to reconcile with the church. So how can this be seen as a deliberate turn from God? No. No, this does not count as sin. It cannot.

Her head is pounding. She has begun experiencing migraines. Much of her mental energy is spent now on reassuring herself, reminding herself that all her actions are circumstantial. The migraines are sometimes head splitting and debilitating, like someone is hacking with a hoe at the back of her head, felling her to the ground for their own enjoyment. They watch her suffer as she tries not to submit to her sense of disappointment in herself. She hopes that eventually she will become numb to the feeling.

Perhaps it's become like this because she now carries the weight of a secret. Her visit to the n'anga. She can't admit to herself that she went of her own accord. She hasn't told Chiedza about their visit to the svikiro either. She takes it to be a secret between husband and wife. Perhaps because she is ashamed and even scandalised that her husband is the type to dabble seriously in mashopeshope. Now this new transgression has been added. She herself sought out the n'anga and her otherworldly forces, without any nudge from Zvobgo. At least, none direct. This had added a new burden for Tsitsi.

She hasn't visited her mother in a week. She has seen Chiedza, but does not want to burden her with this concern. The only other person who knows is Mary, the house girl. What if she tells someone? What if she is spiteful and slips it to Zvobgo?

Until after the son is born, it must be kept a secret. Once

the son is born, she could simply laugh it off as a matter of jealousy, and point to the fact that the house staff have never liked her. He would be too filled with love for his son—and, of course, the mother of his son—to probe any further. Now, in this delicate phase, she couldn't afford any kind of disruption or setback.

Perhaps she should send Mary home? If Zvobgo asks after her, Tsitsi could explain that she had stolen something. But he would surely ask what that was. She would have to throw something away. But then what if it were found by a diligent worker who would then contradict her? Maybe it would be easier if she simply said that Mary confessed that she had got pregnant by one of the house boys next door? But Zvobgo would surely want to confront him and his employer, help her get any damages due to her family. Maybe it would be better if Tsitsi were to claim that the father was a nameless hwindi in town. Yes, Tsitsi could then pre-empt Zvobgo's questions by exclaiming how these rural girls are so fertile and can't keep their legs closed when they come to town. She would go on to exclaim how terrible the hwindis were! Hadn't Zvobgo read those terrible stories about hwindis stripping women wearing mini-skirts? She would explain that she had no choice but to send her home for her own good. Of course, she would send her home with a few boxes of groceries and perhaps $100, $200, even $300. In this economy, isn't that generous? Surely it will suffice as a decent golden handshake? Yes, this is what she will do. And she will do so tonight.

At the office she finds Tabitha at her old desk. Luckily, there is no need for any reconnaissance as she remembers the office well.

How unoriginal, Tsitsi thinks as she eyes her. A low-cut

top, a thin pencil arch hovering over blue eyelids, too-red lipstick for her too-dark skin, oily hair coiffed in a perm maintained by red talons. The sickly sweet notes of her perfume foist themselves into Tsitsi's nostrils. She is wearing the ill-disguised uniform of a temptress.

She takes a deep breath and slows her heartbeat to prevent her voice from betraying her nerves.

"What's the occasion, Miss Mutasa?"

Tsitsi wonders if she has given the girl too much credit. She is not very sophisticated in the way in which she does things. Maybe that is a function of her youth. She is younger than Tsitsi. Being young often does pass for being attractive.

"Mai Zvobgo, the usual—the Book Café. Harare isn't called the city that never sleeps for nothing," says Tabitha.

"I think you should dress more appropriately next time," Tsitsi says through a tight smile.

"Tabitha!" Zvobgo calls loudly from the adjacent boardroom. Tsitsi watches as the girl obediently rises, noting her above-the-knee hemline. She reminds Tsitsi of herself. The comparison simultaneously repels and emboldens her to eliminate her threat.

Tsitsi is behind Tabitha's desk as soon as the girl is out of sight. She turns to wedge her hand between files and places the glass bottle behind the large filing cabinet. She is back in front of the desk before Tabitha returns.

The entire operation feels a little too quick, too easy. There should have been more difficulty, she thinks, a stab of doubt slowly creeping up on her like rust on a council gate.

"I let Mr Zvobgo know that you are here. He can see you now."

"No, don't worry—I see that Zvobgo is busy. I'll see him tonight instead."

Tsitsi turns and leaves quickly. She nods at the guards as they salute again. She prolongs the push of her right thumbnail into the car remote, while her left hand sweats around the curves of the door handle. Once inside the car, she reclines into the leather seat and sighs, releasing a gust of residual anxiety.

Safe in this cocoon, she decides to make a final wager with God. This is the first and last time she will resort to such means. All she needs is to fall pregnant with a son and all will be well again. That's all. Really, it is.

24

Tsitsi and Zvobgo are driven not unceremoniously along the brick-paved driveway skirting Holy Trinity Catholic Church. On their way, they scatter unsuspecting motorists, cyclists and pedestrians.

"What did I tell you, Comrade?" Zvobgo chuckles on the phone. "Yes, we have nothing to worry about. Nyika ndeye ropa! We have emerged the victors once again."

The couple alight from the Prado as Kasongo places himself at the church entrance. They stop mid-entry in the doorway of the light airy church, surprised to find a service is underway.

"Mea culpa, Mea culpa, Mea maxima culpa," the congregation murmurs after the priest, faithfully enacting their religious rites.

Tsitsi's shoes, though only slightly heeled pumps worn to evoke a vestige of humility and grace, clip-clap audibly on the stone floor. A few congregants turn back to survey the disturbance. The rest remain in prayer, diligent in their commitment. Tsitsi recognises the comical cadence of the priest's voice. It belongs to Fata Marwira, ever the stern-faced minister, at the pulpit. She smiles as she remembers his fanatical use of Latin.

"Argh, Mrs Chimombe again! That old woman gave us the wrong appointment time! I've never had such an absent-minded secretary," Zvobgo hisses.

Tsitsi places her hand on the small of Zvobgo's back, playfully restraining his anger and perhaps also restraining herself from showing too much visible pleasure at Tabitha's replacement. "We can't leave now—we are already here. We can wait in the vestibule until Fata Marwira has finished the service."

She leads Zvobgo into the foyer. She gingerly hikes up the floor-length skirt of her elaborate cream African attire as she bends to take a seat on a wooden bench. All the while hearing the congregation's call and response and enjoying it. This particular one is triadic, beginning with Fata Marwira, followed by the voices of the parish before coming together in reconciliation.

Fingers shuffle through the pages of the hymnal as Fata Marwira intones the liturgy with nasal piety. For many, this is little more than a gesture; the liturgy had been heard and repeated so often it is now a weathered inscription in their hearts. Tsitsi feels she has missed its familiarity. She feels an affinity with this rigid routine and procedure.

Fata Marwira adjusts his collar and now stresses the words: "Therefore I beseech the blessed Mary, ever Virgin, blessed Michael the Archangel, blessed John the Baptist, the holy Apostles, Peter and Paul, all the saints, and you, Father, to pray to the Lord our God for me. Amen."

The service ends and the parishioners trickle out. Fata

Marwira remains at the altar. The altar boys busy themselves with the tidying up of the church.

Tsitsi hikes her skirt back up and gestures for Zvobgo to stand. Noticing the movement in the vestibule, Fata Marwira stands with his arms flung open, mirroring the crucified Jesus that towers above him as he beckons Tsitsi and Zvobgo.

"Let us go to my office."

He brings out his best non-communion wine, a fine sherry, and pours two glasses. Tsitsi politely declines.

"How may I be of service to you?" Before they can answer, he continues, "It's getting to be so busy these days. It seems people are finding God again. People who had known the church in their youth or those who simply like this monument of a building, or return to it for funerals. Sometimes their children get married here."

Tsitsi nods. "Fata, we have come to find out about dates for a wedding this year? We know it will be a tight fit."

"Ah, a holy union. I have had the privilege of conducting the sacrament of marriage for over forty years, and have counselled many couples. Difficult at times, yes, but alas, amor vincit omnia."

"Yes, Fata," Tsitsi nods and smiles at Zvobgo.

She looks up at the portrait of the Archangel Michael defeating Lucifer, then at Zvobgo who is facing the priest. She grips the pouch in her handbag. As if willed by her action, Zvobgo looks at her. Discreetly placing a hand on her belly, he adds, "We know it might be imprudent because of the rainy season, but we're thinking of a summertime wedding. Do you have any openings in December?"

ACKNOWLEDGMENTS

After some years of writing and editing non-fiction and fiction, I can say there is nothing more personal for me than letting someone into your imagination; nothing makes me feel more naked in the public eye. I am naked as I give birth to a baby which has been in the womb for nearly five years, with very uneven growth spurts and strange ways of kicking stomach walls for its mother's attention. Without belabouring the metaphor, there are several who have been midwives and midhusbands.

Ndinotenda, Mama and Deddie, my brother Farai Chigumadzi, mhuri yese yekwaChigumadzi neyekwa-Chiganze.

Ndinotenda, my confidants Thato Magano and Sizwe Thandukwazi Nxumalo who go through this life thing with me every day.

Ndinotenda, the late Sekuru 'Teacher' Chiganze. One of the earliest moments of my 'seriously engaging' literature was of the Shona books that my grandfather, a retired primary schoolteacher in Zimbabwe, would buy and send for me to read.

Ndinotenda, Aus' Thabiso for taking the chance.

Amai Zukiswa Wanner, Amai Danai Mupotsa, Ntate Mandla Langa, Ntate Raks, BM (Bongani Madondo), Ntate Sandile Ngidi and Mukoma Tinashe Mushakavanhu.

Ndinotenda, Sean Fraser for being so gracious and patient in the process and Aus' Lebo Mashile for making the connection.

Ndinotenda, Shireen Hassim and Pumla Dineo Gqola, for your example and your willingness to help us along.

Ndinotenda, roomiza Sisipho Moorosi, Nombuso Nkambule, Andiswa Maqutu, Cédric Ntumba, Vanessa Malgas, Sindi Kwenaite, Tamara Paramoer, Tumisho Grater and Tariro Muzenda, who all read when the story was just a short story.

To you all: Ndinotenda zvikuru.

ABOUT THE AUTHOR

Panashe Chigumadzi was born in Zimbabwe and raised in South Africa. She is the founding editor of Vanguard magazine. A columnist for The New York Times and contributing editor to the Johannesburg Review of Books, her work has featured in titles including The Guardian, Chimurenga, Washington Post and Die Zeit. She is a doctoral candidate at Harvard University's Department of African and African American Studies. Sweet Medicine (BlackBird Books, 2015) was her debut novel and won the 2016 K. Sello Duiker Award. Her second book, These Bones Will Rise Again, a reflection on Robert Mugabe's ouster, was published in June 2018 and was shortlisted for the Alan Paton Award for Non-fiction.

Other Blackbird Books available in North America through Rising Action

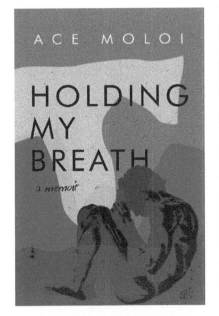

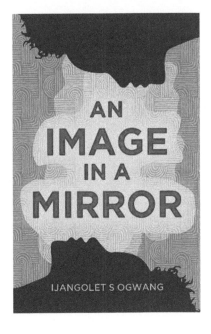